Story by Mariah Marsden and Brandi Handley

with contribution from Josh Elder

Andrews McMeel
Publishing®
a division of Andrews McMeel Universal

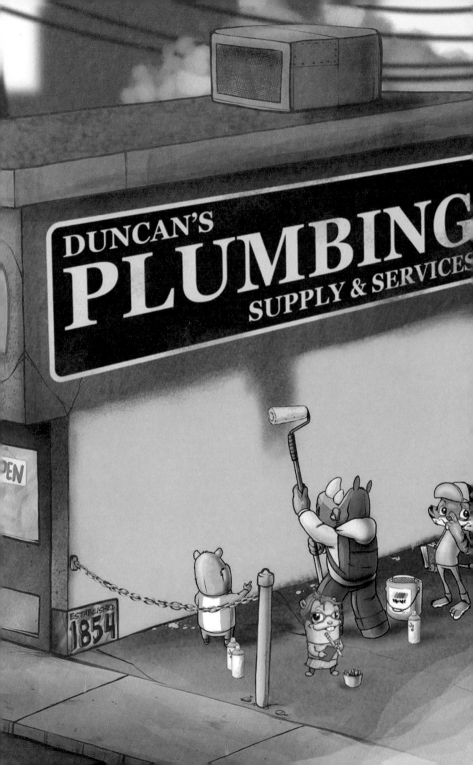

The three boys stared blankly at the blank wall, and the blank wall stared blankly back at them.

"Are you three just going to stare at that wall all day or are you actually going to paint?" asked Phlox Prairie. The reporter-in-training was writing a story on the mural project for the school newspaper. "How am I supposed to convey the excitement of watching paint dry if no paint is ever painted?"

"First, we have to decide what to paint," said Rumpus. "It has to be something unique. Something no one has ever seen before." Rumpus Horn was as hardheaded as he was bighearted. He always fought for what he thought was right. In other words, he was stubborn.

"In my opinion, it should be a scene drawn from nature, something authentic. A vision of tranquility in the center of the city."

Tai Bengali was the brains of the trio, as well as Phlox's partner on their championship sixth-grade mathletics team.

"You gotta be kidding me, Tai," said Phil Prairie, Phlox's twin. "I mean, you want people to actually look at this thing, right? That means you need action! Excitement! Danger!" He himself was a prairie dog of action, and, according to his friends, a little too easily excited.

The three boys had been best friends since kindergarten, where they bonded over crayons, finger paint, and snack time. The interest in art stuck, and over the years, each developed his own unique style: Tai strove to make his drawings

as realistic and accurate as possible, Rumpus invented strange animals and crazy weapons, and Phil's paintings practically leapt off the paper with action and adventure.

Between them, they had produced thousands of drawings and hundreds of paintings. But this was their

first mural, and their first time working together on an art project, so things were off to a rocky start. The only suggestion by Rumpus's grandfather, whose wall they were painting, was that the subject be something from the Wild West. From there they were free to do anything they wanted—which meant that from there, they parted ways.

"Why don't you three compromise and paint all that stuff in together?" Phlox suggested.

A booming voice answered, "Now that's a fine idea." It was Rumpus's grandfather, Duncan Horn, owner of Duncan's Plumbing Supply & Services. He walked out of the doorway of his shop, plunger in hand.

Grandpa Duncan had been a plumber in Kansas City for almost forty years, and his shop carried every kind of pipe, faucet, and fixture that you could imagine. Grandpa Duncan took the same kind of pride in his work that his grandson took in his art, because to Grandpa Duncan, plumbing was an art.

"Each of you has your own ideas," Grandpa Duncan said as he dropped paint cans at the boys' feet. "I get that. But sometimes things—like this here mural—are just too big for any one person to do alone. You have to work together. You know, it's a lot like plumbing."

The kids had to stifle a groan because Grandpa Duncan thought everything was like plumbing: soccer tournaments, science fair projects, camping trips . . . the list went on.

"In a house, you have pipes running every which way. And when the system is working the way it should, you can take a shower at the same time your mother is running the dishwasher. But if just one pipe gets clogged, all the pipes in the house can back up."

Grandpa Duncan concluded without missing a beat: "And that's why you have to work together. You kids get what I'm saying?"

"Yup . . . Yes, sir . . . Uh-huh," the boys said, not getting what he was saying at all.

"All right, then," Grandpa Duncan grinned. "Let's get this show on the road. You kids brought the talent, and I brought the tools. Some very special tools."

The kids crowded around as Grandpa Duncan began prying open the dusty old paint buckets.

"Whoa . . ." Phil said. It wasn't like any paint they'd ever seen before. The colors were so rich and so vibrant that they almost seemed to glow.

It took a moment, but Phlox's reporter instincts kicked back in: "What kind of paint is this, Mr. Horn? I don't see any labels."

"Oh you can't buy paint like this at any store," Grandpa Duncan said with a twinkle in his eye, opening a big box of brushes, rollers, spray paint—everything they needed. "But I have it on good authority that it will really make your artwork come to life."

Rumpus grabbed a brush, dipped it in the paint, and held it aloft: "What are we waiting for? Let's paint a mural!"

The next several hours were a whirlwind of creativity, with only the sounds of *psssht*ing spray paint and the wet slap of paint brushes on concrete. In practically no time at all, the boys had covered most of the wall.

In between visits to the shop to ask Grandpa Duncan questions, Phlox took her turn filling in areas with art inspired by his answers. According to Grandpa Horn, back when he was a boy his own grandfather

told him stories about the days when Kansas City was the gateway to the Wild West.

Right where they lived was the place where wagon trains began their great journeys on the Santa Fe, California, and Oregon trails, where the Pony Express established its first station for riders carrying mail and packages all the way to California in ten days flat, and where the railway lines met to connect the great cities of the east with the untamed wilderness of the west.

"I'm counting on you kids," Grandpa Duncan had told her, "to make a mural that will transport you to the Old West the same way my grandfather's stories transported me."

Phlox backed up to take a look at the wall. The boys hadn't worked together so much as next to each other. And the mural didn't look like a single painting so much as three vastly different paintings side-by-side. Tai had painted a Western landscape of rugged mountains, dramatic canyons, and vast plains. Phil's portion featured outlaw desperadoes, some wielding snakes as weapons. And Rumpus filled his section with bizarre images like hamster-riding warriors, stampeding cattlefish, and giant tumbleweeds with fangs, to name a few.

Obviously, they had totally missed the point of Grandpa Duncan's speech. Nevertheless, Phlox had to admit that the painting was rather impressive. And odd, the way it sparkled and glowed in the midday sun.

Phil, too, stood back to admire the mural. "Gotta be honest," he said, "I think it's clear that my sections really are the most exciting. Don't you agree, Phlox?"

Tai and Rumpus snorted, but kept painting.

"As a journalist," Phlox said, tactfully deflecting the question, "I have to remain impartial."

"Betrayed by my own sister!" Phil grumbled while his friends laughed.

Phlox swiftly changed the subject: "And as a journalist, it's also my responsibility to properly commemorate this momentous occasion."

She reached into her pocket and pulled out her mini digital camera.

Rumpus, Phil, and Tai groaned. There are few things twelve-year-old boys like less than posing for pictures. Still, this was their first mural, and it really needed to be recorded for posterity. So they grudgingly turned and gave the best fake smiles they could muster.

"Say 'Wild West!'" Phlox said.

"Take the picture!" said Rumpus through gritted teeth. "The paint is drying on my roller!"

She snapped. "Hmmm," she said, looking at the shot. "That didn't come out so well. I'd better try again."

The boys groaned again.

Phlox looked at her camera screen to make sure she had the shot lined up properly. That's when she saw it. The mural appeared to be . . . glowing. Really glowing. And getting brighter by the moment. She let the camera drop to look at the shimmering surface with her own eyes.

"Hey, we still doing this picture thing?" a very annoyed, still-smiling Phil asked.

"Can we at least stop smiling?" Tai asked. "My face is really starting to hurt."

Phlox ignored them. She pointed at the mural. "Am I crazy," she asked, "or do you guys see that, too?"

"See what?" said Rumpus. He and the other boys turned around.

"Oh. That," Rumpus said. The boys stared in awe at the strange sight.

Phlox walked up to the mural and reached out.

"What are you doing?" Tai demanded.

"I just want to . . . touch it," she said. Her eyes were glazed over, almost as if she was mesmerized.

"I think that is a very bad idea," Tai warned. "The paint is still wet—and it's glowing."

"No big . . . deal . . ." she said in a faraway voice.

Her voice trailed off as she touched the wall. It wasn't sticky like she expected. It felt more like the surface of a warm bath. And just like in a bath, her touch sent a ripple spreading out across the mural.

"OK, we're all going crazy," Tai said.

"You guys have to try this!" Phlox said, breaking into a grin. The boys joined in. It was like tossing pebbles into a pond, the ripples overlapping and reflecting off each other to create a kaleidoscope of intersecting circles. It was beautiful, and a lot of fun.

Then Rumpus got a bit too excited and tapped the wall a bit too hard. His fingers broke the surface and went into the wall. He immediately yanked them back out again, but when he saw they were fine, Rumpus pushed his arm in all the way up to his elbow. That's when he realized his arm was through the wall and out the other side. He could feel a breeze—a hot, dry breeze—on his hand.

"I think there's something here!" Rumpus exclaimed.

"Yeah, the inside of your grandpa's shop," said Phil.

"No, something . . . different," Rumpus replied. "I'm going to find out what it is."

Before his friends could respond, Rumpus simply walked straight into the mural. It shimmered and rippled around him as he passed through.

And just like that, he was gone.

And just like that, Rumpus was back!

Phlox, Phil, and Tai gasped in unison as Rumpus, still on the other side of the mural, stuck his head back through to the Kansas City side.

"Guys, I'm in the mural!" the rhino exclaimed.

"Yeah, we can see that," said Phil.

"No, I mean I'm actually in the mural. The picture we painted? It's a real place, and I'm standing there right now. You've got to come and see for yourselves."

With that, Rumpus disappeared back into the painting, leaving his friends to debate whether or not to follow.

"No. No way. Not a chance," Tai said, shaking his head emphatically.

"You're overthinking it," Phil said. He turned to his sister. "Come on, sis," he said as he jumped in.

Tai turned to Phlox, hoping she would listen to reason. "Phlox, you can't think that this is a good idea."

"What I think is, this story just went from the arts section to the front page," she answered. Then she, too, strode into the painting.

"I know I'm going to regret this," Tai muttered. Then he took a deep breath, walked up to the mural, stuck his right foot in, and slowly slid through.

Tai found himself standing at the foothills of a mountain range looking out over vast desert plains. It was like nothing he'd ever seen before, yet it was also incredibly familiar—it was the very same landscape he'd painted in the mural.

In the distance rose a giant mountain range of countless peaks and valleys. And right behind him,

at the base of a foothill, was a bright, glowing, blank space the exact size of their mural. It was the back of the mural and the other side of the portal they had just come through—which meant it was probably their only way back home.

"Welcome to the other side, buddy!" Rumpus called in a loud voice.

As Rumpus, Phil, and Phlox walked toward him, Tai observed that each step they took left strange smudges in the dirt, like they were stepping in mud even

though it was very sunny in the middle of the desert. This got Tai thinking. He reached out and touched the rock wall beside the mural and found that it was damp and sticky, and left what looked like globs of reddish-brown paint on his fingers. Tai found this strange, and a theory began to form in his mind.

While Tai conducted his experiments, Phlox conducted a bit of business.

"I told you he'd come through," Phlox said to her brother. "Now pay up."

"All right, all right," Phil said as he dug through

his pocket to produce a wadded-up dollar bill, which he reluctantly handed over. "Just don't spend it all in one place."

"Now that the gang's all here," said Rumpus, "we can do some real exploring!"

"That's fine, because I have a theory I want to test out. But whatever we do it's very important to stay close to the mural," Tai cautioned, motioning back toward the glowing portal. "It's our only . . . way . . . home . . ."

Tai's voice trailed off as he slowly realized that there was nothing there but the plain dusty rock face of the foothill. The mural was gone. Which meant so was their portal back.

"Right, so where is it?" Phil asked, anxiously.

"It was there just a second ago," Phlox said in a daze, looking just as anxious as her brother.

"I said this was a bad idea," Tai said, quickly panicking. "I knew something like this would happen."

Rumpus turned to Tai, trying to reassure his friend.

"Yes, you did, but you also said you had a theory. Maybe that can help us."

"My theory, of course . . . So, um, when all of you were walking, you left smudges on the ground. As if the ground was wet and muddy, even though we're in the middle of the desert where it likely hasn't rained in months," Tai started.

"Yeah, I noticed that, too," Phlox said.

"And when I touched the rock face, it was wet and sticky. Some of it even came off on my hand," Tai continued, holding up his paw for all to see—the fur was matted with reddish-brown gunk.

Rumpus reached out to touch the rock. "Well, it's dry now."

Tai nodded. "The rock face is dry and now the portal is gone," Tai continued, gaining confidence and energy the more he explained his theory. "It was the paint drying!"

He turned to Phlox. "When did you first notice that the painting was glowing?"

She thought for a moment and then said, "I guess it was right after you guys had finished the mural. Before the paint dried."

"So as long as the mural was still wet and unfinished, we could pass through it. But as soon as it dried, the mural was complete and we were sealed into the world inside the painting."

"So how do we get home?" Rumpus asked.

"I . . . I haven't figured that part out yet," Tai replied.

"Great. Whole lotta good that does us," Phil complained.

"Actually," Phlox interjected, pointing toward the thick cloud of dust billowing over the horizon and headed straight toward them, "right now, I think we need to run!"

The cattlefish were the size and speed of small cars, and the herd swam through the air the way a school of fish swims through the sea—fast and furious. They were absurd, adorable, and utterly terrifying.

"Run! RUN!!!" yelled Phlox.

"No kidding! But where to?" Phil asked.

"Higher ground!" Rumpus said, pointing up the mountain. "We can't outrun them. We'll have to get above them!"

Phil and Phlox quickly scampered up the steep foothill and onto a nearby ridge, out of harm's way. Tai followed, his tiger agility allowing him to leap to safety.

Rumpus was not so fortunate. He had never scampered up anything in his life and rhinos weren't exactly known for their agility.

"You're going to have to pull me up!" Rumpus yelled.

"With what?" Tai yelled back.

"There has to be something up there!" Rumpus yelled, glancing back at the charging cattlefish.

Tai lowered a stick.
Phil grabbed Tai's tail and
Phlox grabbed Phil. The three pulled
with all their might. Together they managed to haul
Rumpus up to the ridge just in time. The cattlefish
stampeded beneath in a large cloud of dust.

"I always say I only like my fish shaped like sticks,"
Phil said, still catching his breath.

"I bet those fish will be talking for weeks about the big rhino that got away," joked Rumpus.

The friends cracked up, relieved at their escape. Phlox walked to the edge of the ridge, snapping pictures.

"What are you doing?" Tai asked.

"I have to have photos to illustrate the story I'm writing when we get back home," Phlox said.

"How are we going to get back home?" said Phil.

"We'll find a way," Rumpus said. "Somehow."

"Um, I think you three are going to want to see this," said Phlox. She had something in her hand.

"Whoa! Is that what I think it is?!" Phil said, trying to snatch it. "Let me at it!"

"May I?" asked Tai.

Phlox handed over the apple-sized object to Tai.

"Yellow color, heavy, dense . . ." Tai murmured. He bit into it, leaving a fang impression. ". . . and yet relatively soft. I can't say for certain without running a nitric acid test, but I feel confident that this is . . ."

"Gold!" Phil exclaimed, snatching the nugget.

"We're rich!" Phil shouted, bouncing and cartwheeling around Rumpus. "Do you know how many paintbrushes this will buy us? How many cans of spray paint? How many—"

"We get it," said Rumpus. He tried to snatch the gold nugget from Phil.

"I wouldn't say we were rich exactly," said Tai. "One ounce of gold is about $1,000 these days and I'd estimate this piece is one-fifth or one-sixth of an ounce, so this would get us around $200. But it's likely there's more out here."

"There has to be," Rumpus said. He spotted a trail leading away from the edge of the foothills and up into the mountains ahead of them. "Let's check it out."

"Am I imagining things, or is that mountain sparkling?" Phlox said, aiming her camera. "It's beautiful!"

"Thanks," said Tai. He recognized the landscape as the one he had painted in the mural. "I highlighted the reds and browns with gold paint."

"Way to go, Tai!" Phil said, gazing at the shimmering mountains. "We're going to be so rich!"

"I wouldn't count on it," said a sharp voice behind them. "Stop where you are and turn around."

The four friends turned slowly and came face to face with a large hawk as tall as Rumpus. The hawk snatched the gold nugget from Phil's hand with his curved beak.

"Hey! That's ours!" Phil blurted out. But the gold was already out of sight, hidden among the hawk's full feathers. Across his broad chest was a strap attaching a quiver filled with arrows.

"No," the hawk said, gazing at each of them in turn with his unblinking eyes. "Nothing here belongs to you. You're standing west of Pleasant Junction. And everything west belongs to the Claw Foot Tribe. All of

it." The hawk closed his beak with a snap, making Tai, Phil, Phlox, and even Rumpus jump.

"We're re-really sorry, sir," Phlox stammered. "We didn't mean to trespass."

"Another of the Badger's expeditions, no doubt," said the hawk. "He's been sending thieves to steal our gold for months. Well, it stops now."

"We didn't mean to steal from you. We don't even know any badgers—" Tai started.

The hawk snapped his beak together once more, silencing Tai.

And then, from high above,
a great owl soared down
to land in a crouch.

His headdress bobbed as he walked with an arrogant stride. He passed the hawk with a nod before sizing up the four friends. He glared at them. "That's enough. You're coming with me and that's final." The owl leaned closer to show off a long, razor-sharp talon he handled like a dagger. "I'm called Chief Talon for a reason." He pointed the talon at Tai. "Would you like to find out why?"

Wide-eyed, Tai shook his head.

"Oh, yeah?" Rumpus said, stepping forward. "There's only two of you and four of us. Let's go, guys." He started to turn away, pulling Phil along with him, when the shadows of the mountain crags started to move.

Armed war hawks stepped out of the shadows and perched at the edges of the cliffs. Dark shapes whirled above them. Sharp piercing screams of what sounded like hundreds more hawks surrounded the four friends. "Let me guess," Rumpus said to Phil. "You painted war hawks in the mural."

Phil shrugged sheepishly. "What can I say? I love an adventure."

From behind Chief Talon another owl appeared. She was very small and dressed in Native American garb similar to Chief Talon and the war hawks. She squinted in the bright sun, examining the four friends.

"Wait, Chief," she said. "Don't you see?"

"This is not the time, Bright Eyes," said Chief Talon. He made a signal with his right wing and the war hawks circling above them began to descend.

"A rhinoceros, a tiger, and a pair of prairie dogs—one girl and one boy," Bright Eyes said excitedly.

"You know I don't believe in prophecies!" Chief Talon exclaimed. "They're trespassers and thieves—nothing more!"

"They must be taken to Grandmother Buffalo," Bright Eyes insisted. "They may hold the key to understanding the mystery of the caves."

Chief Talon and Bright Eyes stood talon to talon, staring each other down. Phlox wondered how that little owl could be so brave to stand up to the Chief. And what was the owl talking about anyway? Prophecies? Mystery? Caves?

But going to see whoever Grandmother Buffalo was sounded far better than whatever Chief Talon had in mind. Bright Eyes seemed authoritative somehow, even wise. Phlox admired her and already trusted her.

"Psst." Phlox heard Rumpus behind her. He slipped a can of spray paint from his backpack into her hand. He, Phil, and Tai were each armed with spray paint, too.

"That is a really bad idea," Phlox whispered. "Besides, I think Bright Eyes is trying to help us."

"I'm not taking any chances," Rumpus hissed. "We need to create a distraction."

The war hawks circling above them seemed to be in some kind of holding pattern. Phlox kept watching Bright Eyes. It seemed as though Bright Eyes's head was cocked to one side. In fact, it kept nodding—sharply—to the left. Was this some kind of signal? Phlox looked to where Bright Eyes appeared to be motioning and noticed a large boulder several yards away.

"Guys!" Phlox hissed. "Over there!" Phil, Tai, and Rumpus spotted the boulder and nodded in agreement. Some form of cover was better than nothing.

"On three," Rumpus whispered. He and Tai and Phil shook their spray cans furiously, getting ready to blast paint at Chief Talon, but at the first sound of rattling, the war hawks screeched in alarm.

"Wha—Where did you get those?" cried Chief Talon.

"We're artists!" Phil yelled. He and Tai and Rumpus pressed as hard as they could on their spray cans, shooting powerful jets of paint into the air. Chief Talon flew up in alarm as the four friends ran for the boulder.

Rumpus turned to release one more spray of paint, but there was no need. The war hawks had leapt into the air and were wheeling in panicked circles high above them. Rumpus looked down to see why: On the ground before him was a creature resembling a snake, but whose body was made up of parts of a spray can.

It was the rattle-can snake he'd painted in the mural. As the snake slid away, it rattled its tail, making a sound exactly like a can of spray paint being shaken. When the snake hissed it was the *psssht* of a spray can spraying, and instead of venom the snake spat purple paint. "*Whoa*, amazing!" Rumpus said, "I didn't know it could do *that*." He joined his friends behind the boulder.

"What was that?" asked Tai.

"Just another of my awesome creations!" said Rumpus with a grin.

"I knew she would help us!" Phlox said happily, as their eyes adjusted to the dark behind the boulder.

"She *who*?" said Phil. "That escape was all *us*!"

"Bright Eyes," Phlox said. "She was directing me to this boulder. I think we can trust her. Look, there's a tunnel. Come on!"

The four friends heard the *whoosh* of wings swooping closer. They had no choice but to duck into the tunnel. In the pitch dark Phlox didn't see the steep drop-off. She tumbled down into a cave and landed with a smack. "My arm!" Phlox yelped.

"Phlox!" cried Tai and Rumpus. Following the sound of her voice, they jumped down beside her and pulled her to her feet.

"Sis!" cried Phil. "Are you OK?"

"I don't know," she answered. "My arm really hurts. I think it's broken."

"Some help Bright Eyes was!" Phil said. "She probably led us straight into a trap and now you're hurt."

"I assure you that was not my intention." Bright Eyes stepped out of the shadows. "Let me see your arm." She fluttered to Phlox and held Phlox's injured arm gently in one of her wings.

"How did you get in here?" said Phil. "Stay away from her!"

"Yeah, we don't need your help," said Rumpus.

"*I'd* like her help," said Phlox. "Thanks, Bright Eyes."

Bright Eyes took a bandage from her satchel and began wrapping Phlox's arm. Phlox winced but didn't make a sound. "I've seen the four of you before," Bright Eyes said. "We've been waiting for you to come."

"What are you talking about?" Phil said. "Do you know what you're doing? Where did those war hawks go? Are they going to eat us? How do we get out? . . ."

"Shut up, Phil," said Rumpus. "Answer his first question," he said to Bright Eyes. "We have no idea what you're talking about. All we want to do is get out of here and go home."

"I can help you with that," Bright Eyes said. "But first, you have to help me and the rest of the Claw Foot Tribe."

"Why should we?" Phil said. "We don't even know you."

"Because you're meant to," said Bright Eyes. "There is a prophecy painted on the walls of Talking Rock Caves. It says four strangers are to come and reunite this land."

"And you think that's us?" Tai asked.

"I am almost certain you are the four, but Grandmother Buffalo will know for sure."

"Chief Talon wasn't too happy to see us," said Rumpus.

"I am Chief Talon's daughter," Bright Eyes began.

"I *knew* this was a trap!" Phil said.

"My father is determined to protect our tribe and way of life." Bright Eyes explained. "He is a good Chief, but he is stubborn. That often blinds him to the bigger picture. He sees every new or strange thing as a threat. Even things that may have been sent to help. Like you."

"We're as new and strange as it comes," said Rumpus.

"And we have no idea how to help you," said Phlox.

"My father wants to do what is right," Bright Eyes answered. "I just have to convince him this is the right path. But right now you four need to meet Grandmother Buffalo. She will know what to do next."

"Why should we listen to you?" Phil said, unconvinced. "You're one of them."

"The war hawks aren't the only ones you have to worry about," Bright Eyes said. "The Badger will be after you once the word spreads of your arrival."

"Oh, great," Phil said. "Now a badger is after us."

"Who's this badger?" Tai asked.

"I don't have time to explain," Bright Eyes said, looking worried. "The war hawks will find this cave any minute. We must go."

"I don't think we have a choice," Rumpus said. "We need help."

"Rumpus is right," Tai said. "We have no chance to escape the war hawks on our own."

"Tell us what to do," Rumpus said to Bright Eyes.

Bright Eyes finished wrapping Phlox's arm. "How does it feel?"

"Better," Phlox said. "It still hurts, but it's better."

"Good," Bright Eyes answered. She turned to Rumpus, Tai, and Phil.

"Hide out in Pleasant Junction for now, to get the war hawks off your trail. Then you must get to the Talking Rock Caves. For now, follow me."

They followed Bright Eyes out of the cave and into a steep, narrow canyon, passing under arch after arch of sandstone. There were so many twists and turns and branching passages that they would never have found their way out if it weren't for her. When they finally reached the end of the canyon, Bright Eyes pointed to a chasm. "Follow that path until you reach the badlands."

"Badlands?" said Phil. "That doesn't sound too promising."

"From there you can reach the open desert where the war hawks won't follow," continued Bright Eyes. "On your way to Pleasant Junction, help will find you."

"I thought we couldn't outrun the war hawks," said

Rumpus, hearing their now familiar screeches in the distance.

"You can't," Bright Eyes said. "That's why you'll be riding those." She pointed up the path to where three gigantic hamsters were saddled up and waiting.

"There are only three of them," said Tai. "And four of us."

"Phlox is coming with me," she answered.

"Say what?" Phil cried, indignant.

"No way," Rumpus said. "The four of us stay together."

"Phlox's arm is broken," Bright Eyes said. "Grandmother Buffalo can heal her. In the meantime, you three need to get to Pleasant Junction. There are people on our side there. We'll need their help."

"Uh-uh," Phil said, crossing his arms. "I'm not leaving my sister with you."

"Bright Eyes is right," Phlox said. "I should go with her."

"No way, Phlox," said Phil.

"I'll be fine," said Phlox. "We need answers. Grandmother Buffalo may know how we got here and how to get us home. You guys can meet me there when it's safe. Besides, how can I pass up getting the scoop on such a great story?"

After a long pause, Rumpus said, "It may be the only way."

"Rumpus!" Phil protested.

"Phlox and Bright Eyes are right," Tai said. "We have to trust them. Both of them."

Phil nodded glumly.

"Go east until you get to Pleasant Junction," said Bright Eyes. "You can't miss it."

"Uh, which way's east?" Rumpus said.

Bright Eyes looked at him questioningly.

"We're from the city. We follow street signs, not sun and stars," he said, shrugging.

"That way," Bright Eyes said, pointing.

"Take care of her," Phil said.

"I will. I promise," Bright Eyes said. "When you get to Pleasant Junction, stay out of sight as much as you can. Neddy will help." With that, Bright Eyes and Phlox disappeared back into the tunnel.

"Who's Neddy?" said Tai.

"Beats me," said Rumpus. "Well, giddyup," he said, eyeing the hamsters. "Do either of you know how to ride one of these?"

Hamster-back riding was a surprisingly bumpy experience. Rumpus was jostled from side to side, looking seasick as he gripped the saddle horn for dear life. Tai rode his hamster as if he'd been doing it for years, thanks to his great feline balance.

"They smell like hamster cages," Phil whined. "And this one looks a little like my Uncle Jim. It's kind of freaking me out. You couldn't have drawn something cooler, Rumpus? Like . . . mountain lions? Mountain lions are the way to go."

"Enough with the art criticism," Rumpus grumbled. "I doubt you'd enjoy riding a mountain lion, Phil."

Tai's sensitive ears picked up a noise behind them. He scanned the high canyon walls. It was steep and rocky around them, with lots of boulders and ledges

that seemed perfect for hiding. "Maybe we should go a little faster," Tai said.

"Are you kidding?" Rumpus looked pained as he barely kept from sliding off for the fifth time.

"Mountain lions would definitely be a smoother ride," Phil continued smugly.

Tai heard the strange sound again. Before he could shout a warning, something *whoosh*ed right past his head and hit the canyon wall beside him.

Phil turned and looked. "Is that . . . a paintbrush?"

"Go!" Tai shouted as the air filled with fast-flying paintbrushes. "We've got company!"

Dozens of war hawks raced along the rocky ledges of the canyon, screeching battle calls. "Fire your artrows, braves!" they cried. "Don't let them get away!"

Suddenly, something thunked into Tai's hamster. One of the strange arrows—the artrows—was stuck to the hamster's side, smeared with paint and feathered at the other end. The bright blue color of his mount began to melt ever so slowly, and the hamster began to soften and collapse under him.

"Something's happening!" Tai shouted, but by then his hamster was stumbling, then melting in a pile of wet paint. The other hamsters slipped in the spreading paint, bumping into each other and dumping their riders into the puddle of blue. Paint coated the friends as the remaining hamsters ran around a curve and out of sight.

"What is this?" Rumpus said, wiping his face in disgust.

"It was my hamster, before it got hit with one of their artrows," Tai said. "The artrows must act almost like paint thinner."

"But what will happen to us?" Phil asked uneasily. "Will we turn into puddles?"

"I'm not sticking around to find out," Rumpus said. He ducked as yet another artrow flew at them. "If we make it there," he pointed at a narrow path ahead, "it'll be too tight for their bows to do much good."

Tai and Phil followed, Tai nimbly avoiding holes and boulders while Rumpus barreled right through them. Phil darted between his larger friends, picking up speed as they reached the narrow opening. Tai glanced back to see the hawks circling the blue puddle.

They kept running—down steep hills, across gentler slopes, and finally across the flat, hot ground of the desert.

"Bet you wouldn't mind a hamster now, huh?" Rumpus gasped.

Phil ignored him, smacking his dry mouth. "Tai, tell me we're heading east."

"This is the way that Bright Eyes directed us," Tai said slowly. "But . . . I don't think we're out of trouble just yet."

"War hawks?" Rumpus straightened up, ready for a fight.

"Artrows?" Phil said, light on his toes.

"Nope," Tai said and pointed ahead of them. "Smoke."

Sure enough, they spotted a small fire with a thin bit of smoke rising into the sky. Someone was moving around the fire, but it was too far for the boys to make out who, or what, it was.

"Do you think that's Bright Eyes's friend?" Rumpus asked.

"Could be," Tai said. "We can't know for sure."

"I am dying of thirst," Phil said. He was hunched

over, exhausted, now that he knew that there were no more artrows headed his way—for the moment. "I say we investigate."

"Carefully," Tai cautioned.

They soon realized how difficult it was to sneak up on anyone in a desert; there was absolutely nowhere to hide. They settled on Rumpus taking the lead while Phil and Tai walked forward at his sides. They went right up to the smoldering fire and the small figure that was adding a few more logs.

Rumpus cleared his throat.

The figure turned, and they saw it was a scruffy, strangely dressed field mouse. He looked pretty rough, but when he smiled warmly at the boys, they all felt a bit easier.

"Is that the new war paint fashion these days?" the mouse said curiously, gesturing at the hamster paint

that coated the boys. "Bright Eyes didn't say anything about blue this season."

"You know Bright Eyes?" Rumpus asked cautiously.

The field mouse blushed.

"Of course," he said, a little bashful. "How do you think I knew to catch your hamsters when they came running past?" He pointed off to the side, where the two remaining hamsters were tied to a thorny bush.

"I need to let them know you all made it here safely," the field mouse said, walking toward the fire. "Then I'll take you boys to my camp by the river for the night. And you can wash off all that paint."

"Water," Phil said dreamily, swooning just a little bit at the thought.

"What's your name?" Tai asked.

The field mouse straightened proudly. "Edward N. Limburger—the fourth. Everyone calls me Neddy. Or Little Neddy." He flinched. "But please don't use that one."

"All right, Neddy," Rumpus said, "but how are we supposed to let Phlox and Bright Eyes know we're OK? I really doubt we're going to get any cell phone reception out here."

Neddy grinned wide. "Oh, follow me."

He led the boys over to the fire, which was starting

to go out. He fanned the flames until the logs were all blazing and smoke once again began to drift upward.

Shading his eyes from the sun, Neddy pointed out a similar line of smoke high in the mountains. "There's Bright Eyes with her fire, waiting on me to set mine. Now we can talk."

Neddy reached into his rucksack and took out a thick blanket. To the boys' surprise, he flapped it out and held it over the fire. "You see," he said, "you use a blanket to block the smoke, trapping it and shaping it. It's all in the wrists, really." With great flair, Neddy flipped the blanket in a complicated twist, and up floated . . .

. . . a smiley face emoji.

"I'm telling her that we're all good over here," Neddy explained as the boys watched in stunned surprise.

In the distance, another smoky face appeared in a clear wink.

"Incredible!" Rumpus exclaimed.

"But there's just no way this should be possible!" Tai murmured.

"This is one of the least weird things we've seen in this place," Phil said wryly.

With what little smoke was left from the fire he sent up an awkward, lopsided heart.

"Wait, so Bright Eyes is, like, your girlfriend?" Phil wheedled.

"It's . . ." Neddy looked embarrassed. "Um. It's complicated."

Freshly scrubbed, watered, and full of Neddy's "world-famous" barbecue beans, the boys lay on their woven blankets and looked up at the stars. Neddy had promised to take them to Pleasant Junction in the morning. He tossed them some blankets and, humming to himself, went to the fire a little ways away. He sat there hunched over, using the firelight to examine something in a dull pan. Every so often, he'd spin the metal in a flashy twirl.

"So where do you think we are?" Rumpus asked Tai. "Is this the real world?"

"I have a few working hypotheses," Tai answered slowly. "I think the most likely scenario is that we're in some kind of alternate reality."

"That's your most likely scenario?" Rumpus said incredulously.

"Think about it—we're here in a place that can't possibly exist, filled with creatures and objects that defy all logic," Tai said.

"You know what? It doesn't matter," Rumpus said. "It could be an alternate reality or we could really be here for real. There's no way for us to know. So we have to act like everything is real, or we could get into real trouble."

"Do you guys think this Grandmother Buffalo really knows what is going on?" Phil asked.

"Maybe," Rumpus answered. "Bright Eyes seems to think she does, and that's more than any of us can say. So we just need to keep our heads down until we can get to those caves of hers. Now let's get some sleep."

"PAY DIRT!"

All three boys shot up. Neddy was dancing around the fire with utter glee, kicking up his feet and pumping his arm in victory. He laughed and beckoned them closer with a grand flourish.

"Come see my fortune, boys!" he cheered.

The boys gathered around the fire and peered inside the metal pan he held out. Black mud: That was all they saw.

"Wow, that's definitely . . . something," Phil said over Neddy's shoulder. He twirled his finger next to his head in the universal sign for "crazy."

"Do you see my gold?" Neddy asked eagerly. "Right there in the pay dirt?"

Tai squinted and, sure enough, tiny little flakes, no bigger than a grain of rice, glinted in the firelight. Tiny, tiny flakes. Fewer than a dozen of them.

The boys cleared their throats. Tai looked at Rumpus, who subtly shook his head. Best not mention the gold they'd found on the mountain, at least until they understood what Chief Talon was threatening.

"I thought I'd never see another fleck of gold," Neddy continued. "Bright Eyes used to show me the veins in the mountains, back when . . ." He trailed off with a cough. "Anyway, some of it runs out through the underground streams—a small amount, that is."

Neddy watched the flames, deep in thought. "It used to be easy to find handfuls of the stuff, more than my hamster could carry, when Chief Talon welcomed us townspeople in the mountains. He and my dad were friends."

"What happened?" Rumpus asked.

Neddy suddenly looked very sad. "The Badger happened."

"Who is this badger?" asked Phil, throwing his hands in the air in exasperation.

"He's the one who put my father in prison," Neddy said grimly.

"What?!" the three boys exclaimed.

Neddy nodded. "Locked him in and threw away the key. I haven't seen my dad in nearly a year."

"Is the badger the sheriff or something?" Rumpus asked.

"That's the crazy part. My dad, Big Ned, was the sheriff."

"And he was thrown in jail?" Rumpus asked, confused.

"He opposed the mayor. That's the Badger — Mayor Pleasant." Neddy scowled. "All Mayor Pleasant wanted was gold — wanted it bad. He would send his men into the mountains to steal all they could. So Chief Talon closed off the mountain passes. And he told the mayor the next time he saw people taking gold from the tribe's land he would send his braves on the warpath."

"Uh oh," Phil said.

"And now Chief Talon thinks that we're the badger's thieves," said Rumpus.

"Yeah," winced Neddy. "I think we're headed for trouble."

"Uh, we have to go to bed," Phil said abruptly, pulling Rumpus and Tai away. "Long day tomorrow."

"G'night boys," Neddy called after them. "I can teach you how to pan in the morning. It's a great skill to have in this day and age."

Back on their blankets, Phil leaned forward. "I have something I need to tell you."

"What did you do now?" asked Rumpus.

Phil reached into his pocket and pulled out the biggest gold nugget they'd seen yet. "Just happened to find another one of these lying around. In the cave where Phlox broke her arm. There wasn't a lot of time to talk at the moment and I . . . kind of forgot."

"You forgot about the giant nugget you had sitting in your pocket?" Tai accused.

Phil sputtered. "I'm telling you now, aren't I?"

"Should we tell Neddy about it?" asked Tai.

Rumpus thought for a minute before shaking his head. "Not right now. We keep our heads down, like we decided. We'll go to the town and check things out, and hopefully this mystical Grandmother Buffalo, Bright Eyes, and Phlox can fill us in on what's going on here."

"I'd say things aren't looking too bad right now," Phil said happily, pocketing the gold nugget once again. He gave the lump a satisfying pat.

Tai shook his head, but he was smiling. "Go to sleep, Phil. We've got to ride those hamsters bright and early tomorrow."

Rumpus groaned.

WELCOME TO **PLEASANT JUNCTION**

HOWDY!

This way to ➡
QUIET • SAFE • PERFECT

Pleasant Junction was . . . pleasant.

The boys had imagined the typical Old West town: dusty, ramshackle, with stray tumbleweeds and maybe a gunfight or two. But in Pleasant Junction, even the dirt roads were shockingly clean. The houses looked identically spic-and-span, as did the shops. In the center of town, a white marble city hall gleamed in the morning sun. The few people on the streets walked quickly and kept their heads down.

"Did either of you draw this place?" Tai asked.

Phil and Rumpus shook their heads, staring at the spotless town around them.

"Curious . . ." murmured Tai. A theorizing look came over his face.

"You boys need to stay out of sight," Neddy said. He ushered them into a stable, nervously checking the windows and doors. Hamsters shifted in their stalls and made odd squeaking sounds, almost like neighs.

"It smells like hamster pee in here," Phil whined.

Suddenly, there was a loud pounding on the door. "We know you're in there, Little Neddy! Now open up in the name of the law!"

"The law?" Tai asked in an anxious whisper. "Are we in trouble here, too?"

"Everybody's in trouble in Pleasant Junction," Neddy muttered. He gestured to one of the stalls. "Quick—get in there and stay quiet!"

The boys crowded past a big purple hamster and hid themselves in the pile of wood shavings behind him. The shavings were damp and smelly, and the hamster

was even smellier. It kept backing into Phil, who could barely contain his groan of disgust.

"What do we have here, Mongo?" someone sneered as the building door creaked open.

"Hamster stable, Spratt," someone answered in a slow, dumb monotone. "Where hamster ponies live."

"I know that, Mongo, you oaf!" snapped the one called Spratt, rubbing his face. Peering out of the shavings, the boys saw a small, wiry hare wearing a shiny gun belt.

"Mongo sorry," said Mongo. He, on the other hand, was huge, with a beefy body and a dim but sweet expression. Spratt turned to Neddy, oily smile back in place. "We came by earlier, just to check in, but you were nowhere to be found.

Where were you, Little Neddy? Sending smoke signals to that birdbrained girl of yours? Or down in the river, eh? Find anything . . . interesting?"

"I wasn't . . . interesting!" Neddy stuttered.

"You know I'm a deputy, right?" Spratt leaned over the cowering Neddy. "That means that we have the right to take whatever gold you find to Mayor Pleasant for . . . registration. Yeah, registration."

"Yeah, reservation!" Mongo guffawed.

"I'm just training these hamsters," Neddy protested. "Getting them ready for Pleasant Day."

"Is that so?" Spratt said. "Is that why you're so rumpled?" He poked at the field mouse's wrinkled shirt. "And dirty too—isn't he dirty, Mongo?"

"Mongo dirty," the other hare agreed.

"Good grief, not you. Him! He's the dirty one." Spratt turned to Neddy. "That's going to cost you a hefty fee, my friend, for wrinkled clothing. I should add a dirt fee, too, but I'll let it slide just this once."

"Th-thank you," Neddy said, staring at the floor.

"And as for any other . . . activities," Spratt continued, "you know the penalty for smuggling gold, and for talking to Indians. You just watch yourself, Little Neddy, or you'll be sitting in jail like your father!"

Spratt wrinkled his nose in disdain as he gazed around the shabby stables. "But maybe that would be an upgrade, eh?"

"Stinky stables," Mongo agreed. But his eyes were fixed in the boys' direction. They realized in horror that he was grinning at the purple hamster in their stall. He shuffled forward with wide, excited eyes, arms outstretched. "Hamster pony!" he exclaimed. The terrified boys sank deeper into the smelly wood chips.

"Come on, you lug!" Spratt spat, pushing Mongo out the door while Mongo whined about hamster ponies.

The boys emerged from hiding to find Neddy looking shaken. "Well, now you've seen the Wildhare deputies," he sighed. "The mayor's henchmen—dirty, rotten lowlifes. The big one was Mongo. That cannon of his shoots battlebees that are as mean as he is. Luckily, he's dumber than a bag of rocks. The twitchy little one is his brother, Spratt. He's got a mean piranha pistol. I don't advise getting on the other end of that thing. He likes to pretend he's the leader of the gang, when the oldest brother isn't around."

"You mean, there's another one?" asked Tai.

Neddy's scowl would have curdled milk. "Buck Wildhare. The worst of the bunch. We're lucky he wasn't with them."

"What's the deal with this town?" Tai said. "How did such bad guys get in charge?"

"It wasn't always this way," said Neddy. "You might as well hear the whole sad story." He sat down with a sigh and began:

The town wasn't always called Pleasant Junction. Once, it was just Junction—the meeting place of east and west, settlers and natives. The townsfolk lived happily alongside the Claw Foot Tribe, trading with them and traveling freely between mountains and town. Sometimes, there were squabbles—same as in any place—but the folks found a common interest that brought them together: art.

Every year they held a grand art festival where the tribe members and townspeople showed off their projects. Everyone was welcome, and some of the pieces on display were truly weird and wild. The tribe, and one young owl girl in particular, wowed everyone with their specialty: golden art. Painting frames glinted in the sun, statues had golden decorations, and even the paint glittered like it was the real thing.

Sheriff Big Ned Limburger kept the peace. He was respected by everyone in Junction—outside, too. When the notorious Wildhare Gang, a clan of ne'er-do-well desert hares, descended on the region and started robbing trains, banks, and anyone carrying a speck of gold on them, Big Ned and Chief Talon worked together to bring the Wildhares down. The gang had no hope of escape, not with the war hawks high above them

and Big Ned hot on their trail. After that victory, Chief Talon and the sheriff had greater respect for each other than before.

The two became friends, and so did their children, Neddy and Bright Eyes. Bright Eyes showed Neddy the mountain paths and the secret to the tribe's magnificent golden art: real gold.

Times were tough, but they were good. People came from all around for the art festival. Word spread about the Claw Foots' beautiful artwork. That was the beginning of the trouble.

The town started attracting a new kind of character, and in rode Balthazar Pleasant.

He was a fast talker, and he had a lot of cash to spread, although no gold. Pretty soon Balthazar Pleasant owned half the town and the other half was working for him in one way or another. So when he ran for mayor, he won by a landslide.

And why not? He'd helped develop the town, and he'd brought commerce and prosperity. But once he had power, Junction started to change. Not all at once. It was little things at first. The new mayor started passing laws: a penalty fee for littering, which wasn't too bad. Then there was a fine if your storefront was too shabby. Then you received a bill if you failed to wear the right kind of clothing: button-up shirts and carefully ironed pants and skirts. And then the fines got higher, the restrictions got tougher, and pretty soon you couldn't walk through the town without racking up some kind of fine.

But Big Ned was having none of it. When the mayor introduced the new Dirt-Free Bill, which penalized anyone whose clothes or buildings had an "unnecessary" amount of dirt on them, Big Ned laughed right in the badger's face. With

the townsfolk behind him, Big Ned stood up to the mayor and demanded a new election.

The mayor declared that if the lawman would not do his job, he would have to deputize someone who would. And with that, he let the criminal Wildhare Gang free and made the rotten, devious Buck Wildhare sheriff. Mayor Pleasant wasn't particularly fond of the rude, rowdy hare, but he did make a convenient henchman.

Teaming up, these two decided that the best way to take total control of the town was to divide and conquer.

Their first act was to arrest Big Ned for refusing to follow orders. Buck enjoyed that quite a bit, locking up the man who had put him in jail just a while earlier.

And with Big Ned out of the way, there was no one to stop Mayor Pleasant from making the *town exactly how he wanted. He made more ridiculous laws, turned the war hawks and townsfolk against each other, and changed the art festival into the "Pleasant Day" celebration, in honor of himself. Now, he was bringing in investors from the east to pay for more expansion.*

"And so I work here," Neddy said, wrapping up his tale, "shoveling out hamster stalls to pay off my dad's fines."

"That's awful!" Phil said.

"Sometimes I get to the river, like old times." Neddy pulled a small vial of tiny gold flakes from his pocket. "If I can find enough, maybe I can get my dad out of jail sooner. But right now I have to go change my clothes. If those Wildhares catch me in this outfit again, they'll double my fine. You boys can stay here until Bright Eyes gives the all-clear."

When Neddy left, the three boys exchanged a glance.

"I'm curious to see what else is in the town," Tai said. "Because I didn't put any of this in the mural."

"Me neither," Rumpus agreed.

Rumpus, Tai, and Phil tumbled noisily through the
doors of the ice cream saloon, only to find the place
as quiet as a dentist's office, and about as much fun. It
was nothing like the saloons in the Old West movies

the boys had seen. Nobody was dancing or laughing or having any kind of fun whatsoever. Two ground sloths sat together glumly, staring off in different directions. A large tortoise sat at the counter, his head barely peeking out of his shell. An armadillo sat alone at a table sulking in his pickle juice. They all showed only mild interest in the three strangers, glancing up for a moment before sinking back into their gloom.

"This place gives me the creeps," said Tai. "Maybe we should go."

"This whole town gives me the creeps," said Phil. "At least here we can get something to drink."

"OK, well, let's sit over there in the corner," Tai said. "We should at least try to stay out of sight."

"You two grab the table; I'll grab the drinks," said Phil. He strolled over to the counter, hoping to appear like a local. The hammerhead shark behind the counter was rubbing a sparkling clean glass.

"What'll you have?" he asked.

Phil looked around. Most people were having something that resembled radioactive pink lemonade.

"Do you have anything besides whatever that is?" he asked, pointing at the tortoise's magenta glass.

The shark smirked. "We have sarsaparilla for those that can't handle beet juice."

"OK," said Phil. "Three sarsaparillas."

Phil looked around. The only decoration in the place was a large portrait of a badger in a bowler hat. "Is that the mayor?" Phil asked the tortoise.

The tortoise inched his head out of his shell. "Yep," he muttered. He was about to pull his head back in again, but he paused and said, "I'd tell your friends to move if I were you."

"Why's that?" Phil asked.

"That there's the sheriff's table," he answered. "He's due in for his card game any minute now. You don't want to be around when he's ready for cards. You'll have no choice but to play—and you won't win."

"That'll be fifteen cents," said the hammerhead. He slid the foaming sarsaparillas across the counter.

"Oh, um, hang on a sec," Phil said. He felt in his pockets. He'd lost his last dollar in that bet with Phlox about whether Tai would come through the mural or not—which felt like a lifetime ago. The only thing he had on him was the gold nugget from the cave.

"Um, do you take gold?" Phil asked, sheepishly. He set the heavy nugget on the counter with a clunk. All eyes shifted in his direction.

"You better put that away, son," said the shark, eyes fixed on the gold. "Put that away before . . ."

The saloon doors banged open and Sheriff Buck Wildhare sauntered in. His moustache was curled into a sneer and his long ears twitched this way and that. But most frightening was the whip coiled to Buck's belt — a snake whip that constantly hissed and bared very sharp, very real fangs.

Behind Buck followed his bodyguards — Spratt and Mongo. The three came to a sudden stop at the sight of Phil and the gleaming piece of gold.

"Well, well!" said Buck. "I heard there were

strangers about." He leaned on the counter, his hand inches away from the nugget. "Looks like your friends saved us a table," Buck said, pushing Phil before him. "Let's join them, shall we?"

"Visitors in town!" Buck greeted Tai and Rumpus with a chuckle. "We need to give you a proper Pleasant Junction welcome."

"Actually," Tai said, "we were on our way out."

Ignoring him, Buck continued, "That's a mighty impressive chunk of gold you fellas got there. How do three visitors happen upon such a fine specimen?"

"Just lucky, I guess," said Rumpus.

"Lucky, huh?" said Buck. "When I got to this town I spent the entire first year panning." He kept fingering the snake whip. "And I certainly didn't get lucky. I know I look like a stand-up gentleman now."

Phil stifled a snort.

"But there was a time when I woulda robbed a bank to get my hands on a piece of gold that big." He sat forward. "In fact, I did. It was awfully naughty of me, I know," he continued. "But I was desperate. So I can understand your position."

Buck uncoiled the snake whip. It stretched across the table, venomous head pointed at the boys.

"We didn't steal this gold!" Rumpus said. "We found it fair and square."

"I'll tell you what," said Buck. "Let's play for it. Go Cattlefish—the best card game in the west. If you win, you keep your little treasure. If I win . . . well, I'll think of something."

The snake whip kept its eyes on the boys as they arranged themselves around the table.

Rumpus and Phil agreed Tai should be the one to play against Buck. After all, he was the mathletics champion. Buck explained that the object of Go Cattlefish was to match up cards that were alike. It was just like Go Fish except that the deck of cards was about four times as big, which made it more difficult to

find matches. After several rounds, Buck had fourteen matches and Tai had only one. Somehow Buck always knew what was in Tai's hand.

"Come on, Tai!" Phil whispered. "I don't want to find out what Buck has in mind for us if he wins."

"It's hard to beat him when he's cheating," Tai whispered back. "But I think I've figured out a strategy."

He turned to Buck. "Have any hamster cards?"

Grudgingly Buck handed one over, giving Tai his second match. Soon Tai was catching up, with seventeen matches to Buck's eighteen. With fewer cards left in play, Tai's calculations were becoming more and more accurate.

"That does it!" Buck yelled when Tai matched his twentieth pair. "This town doesn't tolerate cheating!" Buck's calm demeanor had evaporated. "Cheating is grounds for arrest!" He snapped his snake whip. The snake hissed, and venom dripped from its fangs.

"Then arrest yourself!" Phil blurted.

Buck stopped cold. "Are you accusing the sheriff of cheating, boy?"

"Er, no—"

"Spratt. Mongo," Buck said. "Arrest these boys, starting with the mouthy little one." Spratt and Mongo stepped forward, handcuffs in their hands.

"Wait!" Rumpus protested. "Take the stupid gold, even though we haven't done anything wrong."

Rumpus tossed the gold nugget at Buck.

"That's a good start," Buck said, stuffing it into his pocket, "but it's a little late for manners." He nodded at Spratt and Mongo to clamp the handcuffs on the boys.

"And here we have the saloon," a booming voice burst through the saloon doors. "The best beet juice in town!"

"Oh, that sounds . . . delightful!" said a second voice—a voice Rumpus, Tai, and Phil immediately recognized.

And sure enough, in came Phlox on the arm of a plump, well-dressed badger who could be none other than Mayor Pleasant himself.

"Oh, look!" Phlox said. "There they are! We should have known they would be here. Investors like to make sure a town has a good watering hole. Besides, they love their sarsaparillas!"

"Hi there, gentlemen," said the mayor, bowing. Phlox shot the boys a look from behind his back that said, *Shhh! Don't say a word.*

Rumpus, Tai, and Phil watched with mouths hanging open as Phlox chatted away with the mayor. She took notes in her notebook while he showed her around. When they arrived at the boys' table, Phlox introduced them: "Mr. Mayor, I'd like you to meet Mr. Horn, Mr. Bengali, and my brother, Mr. Prairie. They're the Kansas City investors you've heard so much about."

The mayor stuck out his hand. It was then that the mayor noticed the shackles on the boys' wrists.

"Looks like we have a situation here," said the mayor. "Buck, what seems to be the problem?"

"These three boys are under arrest," Buck spat.

"Now, Buck," the mayor laughed nervously. "That

just won't do. These aren't just any boys. As Ms. Prairie has just explained, these are the Kansas City investors we've been waiting for. They've got quite a lot of money they'd like to share with our pleasant little town." He chuckled again, trying to clear the tension. "We can't be arresting our wealthy friends here."

"Well, that's funny," Buck said. "They never mentioned that to me." Reluctantly, he nodded at Spratt and Mongo to uncuff the boys.

"You didn't ask," Phil said, rubbing his freed wrists.

"I'm sure this is all just a big misunderstanding," said the mayor. "Ms. Prairie has told me all about their plans to make a large investment." He turned to Phlox. "I'm sure glad you tracked me down, my dear."

"I'm excited to see the rest of your beautiful town, Mr. Mayor," beamed Phlox.

"Well, all right," boomed Mayor Pleasant, "let's hit the dusty trail! Of course, here in Pleasant Junction there is no dust. We have the cleanest streets in the West."

"Come along, boys," called Phlox as she and the mayor trotted out. "You've taken up enough of the sheriff's time. Why don't you tour the town with us?"

After another second of confusion, the three friends grabbed their chance and rushed after Phlox and the mayor into the street.

"It sure is quiet around here," said Tai.

"Our townspeople keep busy," explained Mayor Pleasant. "No time for dawdling."

"Busy doing what?" asked Rumpus.

"Keeping things clean," said the mayor. "And going on expeditions. Explore and expand, I always say!"

"You mean expeditions into the tribe's territory," said Tai. These so-called expeditions must be the bands of thieves Chief Talon had mentioned. By "exploration" the mayor meant finding gold. And by "expansion," he meant taking over the Claw Foot Tribe's land.

"So what are your plans for our investment?" asked Phlox, trying to distract from Tai's accusing tone.

"Glad you asked!" said Mayor Pleasant. They had reached City Hall. "Step into my office, my friends, and let me show you."

City Hall looked like a palace—a big, square, white palace with giant white pillars and huge marble stairs.

"Some office," said Phil. "This place is bigger than the rest of the town put together."

"What he means," interrupted Phlox, throwing Phil a warning look, "is it's very impressive."

"Thank you kindly," said the mayor, pleased. "And your money will go to something even more impressive." He led them to a large, detailed scale model of Pleasant Junction—only in the model, the town spread at least five times beyond its current boundaries, into the Claw Foot Tribe's territory. Worst of all, the tribe's mountains were covered in gold-mining machinery.

"Well?" said the mayor. "What do you think?"

"It's, um . . . big," said Rumpus.

"And impressive," said Phil.

"Precisely!" boomed the mayor. "Now just sit tight. I'll grab the paperwork and we can make a deal!"

As soon as the mayor had left the room, Tai said, "You were great, Phlox! If you hadn't shown up when you did, the three of us would be in jail right now."

"Yeah, Phlox, you're a genius," said Rumpus.

"I was about to handle the sheriff myself," said Phil.

Phlox rolled her eyes. "Good to see you, too."

"Hey, your arm is fixed!" noticed Tai.

"Grandmother Buffalo is an awesome medicine woman," said Phlox.

"How did you find us?" asked Rumpus. "How did you know we needed help?"

"Bright Eyes and I started to worry when nobody returned our smoke signal this morning. Finally Neddy signaled that you guys weren't where he left you."

"We just wanted to look around," said Phil.

"You should have listened to Neddy," said Phlox. "According to Bright Eyes, he knows better than anyone how dangerous this town is. He told Bright Eyes about the investors. She and Grandmother Buffalo suspected that the mayor intends to take over the tribe's land once he gets the money."

"Looks like they were right," said Tai.

"Around here if the mayor thinks you have money, the sheriff can't touch you," said Phlox. "As long as the mayor believes we're the investors, we can buy the tribe some time."

They heard footsteps. A moment later the mayor returned with a stack of papers.

"Here we go, my friends!" said the mayor. "I just need your signatures, then we can start expanding!"

"Actually," said Phlox, "we'd like to talk things over tonight." She inched toward the door. "We think we might have even more money we can invest, but we have to check first."

"Yeah," chimed in Phil. "More money for you."

"Well, in that case," said the mayor excitedly, "you can sign the papers tomorrow morning."

"Uh, sure," said Rumpus. "First thing in the morning."

The four friends turned toward the door but found their way blocked. It was the sheriff.

Sheriff Buck raised his snake whip above his head.
"You four back on up in there," he said.

"Buck!" said the mayor, exasperated. "Now what?"

Buck shot the mayor a glare. "Mayor," said Buck,
"what we have here is four imposters."

Phlox swallowed hard.

"Nonsense!" said the mayor. "You're being
paranoid. Step aside, Sheriff."

"I can prove it," said Buck. Spratt and Mongo came
in, Mongo holding a very small, very frightened field
mouse.

"Neddy!" Tai exclaimed.

The mayor swiveled. "You know this field rodent?"

"Um, well, we've met," Tai admitted.

Tai tried to catch Neddy's eye, but Neddy kept his

head down. He wrung his hat in his hands, twisting and tearing at it.

"Neddy," said Tai. "What's wrong?"

"Go ahead, Little Neddy," said Buck. "Tell everyone what you told me."

Neddy's head practically sank into his hat as he said, "They're not the Kansas City investors."

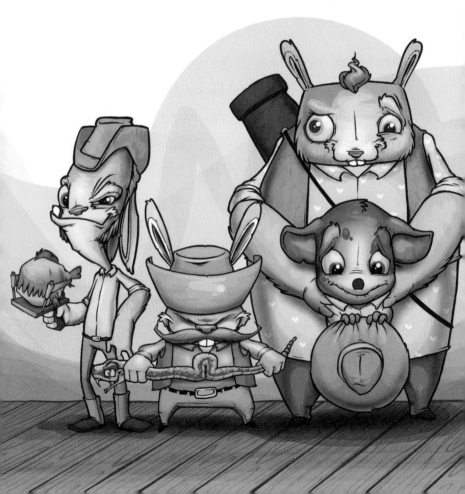

Tai, Phlox, Rumpus, and Phil froze.

"They're liars and cheats!" Buck added.

"No!" Neddy protested. "They're just strangers passing through, that's all."

"Then where did they get this?" Buck pulled out the hunk of gold that he had taken from Phil. "I found this on the little one."

The mayor turned on the four friends: "Have you been stealing my gold?" he demanded. "No one steals my gold!" He snatched the gold nugget from Buck.

The four friends backed away. They were finally seeing what the mayor was really like.

Tai chanced another look at Neddy. The poor mouse looked sick and scared. His eyes were more watery than usual, and his whole body was trembling. His hat was one big wrinkled mess in his hands.

"OK, Little Neddy," Buck scoffed, "get outta here."

"So you won't hurt my dad?" said Neddy. "You said if I helped you, you'd leave him alone."

"Yeah, yeah, sure," Buck said, "we'll leave him alone—so he can rot in jail." Buck laughed, a nasty laugh. "He'll be real safe in there all right. Now run along back to the stables where you belong."

Neddy threw the friends a pitiful last glance before doing as he was told. Tai wanted to go after him.

Rumpus must have been thinking the same thing, because just then he whispered, "We have to make a run for it! Stay behind me." He stepped in front of his friends.

"Imposters!" the mayor exclaimed. "No one makes a fool out of me! Buck, get them out of my sight."

"My pleasure, Mr. Mayor," said Buck.

Right in the second that Buck looked down to reach for his handcuffs, Rumpus lowered his head and aimed his horn at Buck, and behind Buck, the exit. Rumpus snorted once, twice, and charged. Buck and the

handcuffs went flying, and Phil, Phlox, and Tai ran out behind Rumpus. Buck scrambled to his feet, fumbling for his snake whip, but the friends were already racing down the marble staircase.

"Catch them!" Mayor Pleasant called after them.

From behind came a *BOOM*, and a swarm of battlebees buzzed toward them.

"The battlebee cannon!" Rumpus exclaimed. "Run!"

"Where to?" asked Phil. "We can't trust anybody around here. Can you believe that Neddy? You think someone's your friend, they're on your side . . ."

A shot rang behind them—Spratt's piranha gun. A huge school of piranhas zipped through the air. The tiny fish attacked from every side. Even Tai, with his cat reflexes, couldn't swat them away. The bites of their razor-sharp teeth stung and burned.

Pursued by angry bees and ravenous piranhas, the four ran for their lives. The few townspeople on the sidewalk jumped out of their way, but they acted more interested than alarmed. They seemed pleased that Sheriff Buck had to chase his prisoners.

The friends rounded a corner and ducked into the general store. The clerk behind the counter, a chameleon the same color as the wall of beige paint behind him, ignored them.

"Do you think Buck saw us come in here?" Phlox asked.

"I don't know," said Tai. "But it won't take him long to find us."

The clerk looked up. "Running from the sheriff are ya?"

"Kind of," said Rumpus.

"I admire your bravery," said the clerk. "And your stupidity."

"Can you help us?" asked Phlox.

"There's not much I can do," said the clerk, "except point you to the back door."

"We'll take it," said Rumpus.

They followed the clerk down the aisle.

"Isn't that the back door?" Phlox said, as they ran past a door.

"One of 'em," answered the clerk. He led them into an office. He pushed aside a cabinet, and pointed to a small door behind it that blended in with the wall. "From here the train station is just across the street. If you're lucky, you can catch the outgoing train."

Phil and Phlox easily fit through the small doorway, and even Tai squeezed through with little effort. But when it was Rumpus's turn, he let out a snort. "I'm stuck!"

With Phil, Tai, and Phlox yanking and the chameleon clerk shoving, Rumpus finally popped through with a *thwok*.

"Thank you!" called Phlox through the opening.

"I sure hope ya make it," said the chameleon. "You probably won't, but I'll be rootin' for ya."

"The train is here!" said Phil. The four ran.

"But we don't have any tickets," said Tai. "Or money."

"I have an idea," said Phil. He hopped a fence and stood at the last car of the train just as a ground sloth came up dragging a suitcase. With a courteous salute, Phil took the luggage from him and threw it onto the baggage car.

The ground sloth handed over a small piece of gold for a tip and headed to the passenger cars. Phil waved Rumpus, Tai, and Phlox over. The four jumped into the baggage car.

"Nice going, Phil," said Rumpus, settling against a pile of suitcases.

"Yeah, not bad," admitted Phlox.

A whistle blew as the train crawled forward. "I hope we're going in the right direction," said Phlox.

"As long as we're going away from Buck, we're going in the right direction," said Phil.

"We can't just leave," said Tai suddenly.

Rumpus, Phil, and Phlox stared at him.

"Are you nuts?" said Phil. "I'm done with not-so-Pleasant Junction."

"You guys heard Neddy," Tai looked at Phil and Rumpus. "The townspeople are living in fear. They're thrown in jail for wearing wrinkled clothes, or being dirty, or for no reason at all. They have to do whatever Buck and the mayor tell them to do. They're prisoners in their own town!"

"Whoa, easy, Tai," said Rumpus. He and Phil looked at Tai in surprise.

"We have to help them," insisted Tai.

"Grandmother Buffalo and Bright Eyes seem to think that's why we're here," Phlox spoke up. "To help the tribe and the townspeople of Pleasant Junction." She and Tai looked at each other. They both seemed in agreement.

"Whoa, whoa, whoa," interrupted Phil. "Wait just a minute. You're telling me that we're here to help the townspeople *and* the tribe? Aren't they against each other?" There was a long pause. "So how the heck do we do that?"

"I don't know," said Tai, "but Neddy's our friend. We need to help him and his dad and the townspeople get their town back."

"Is he?" Phil argued. "Didn't he just betray us to Buck?"

Just then they all lurched forward as the train braked to a stop with a sudden loud screech.

"We better get out of here," said Phlox. But before they could go anywhere, their boxcar door slid open.

"Nice try," said Buck. "But I run everything in this town, including the trains." With four quick flicks of his wrist, his snake whip left fang marks on the arms of Rumpus, Tai, Phil, and Phlox. For the second time that day, they were handcuffed and led away.

13

"Poor Neddy," Tai said in a gloomy whisper.

"Poor Neddy?" Phil whispered back. "We're the ones stuck in jail!" He pointed out of the tiny cell. "And have you seen our company?"

The jail was as clean as the rest of the town—except for the scruffy-looking inmates of the other cells. One mean-faced fox picked his teeth while his cellmate, a gecko with a hard stare, shuffled a card deck over and over again. "Could you keep it down?" Phlox murmured. "I'm trying to think."

"You expect to think yourself out of this one?" Phil said.

"It couldn't hurt to try, now, could it?" Phlox snapped.

Metal clanged as Jack Rabbit, their jailor, rattled his stick against the bars of their cell. "Quiet down!" he said. The skinny hare was one of Buck's many cousins, and claimed to have been part of the Wildhare gang since back in their bank-robbing days.

"We've been here for hours." Rumpus stood up as he spoke, trying to look intimidating. "When do we get food?"

The jailor laughed and walked away without answering.

From the next cell, a deep voice said: "You're going to be disappointed about the food in this place. Fair warning."

Who was that? The friends could see only darkness between the bars. Finally, they made out a big shape against the far wall.

"Who are you?" Rumpus asked.

The shadow moved forward . . . and shrank, and shrank . . . and shrank. By the time he reached them it had turned into a mouse only a bit taller than Neddy, with a large hat and carrot-red whiskers. "They usually bring food just before sunset," he said with a shrug. "I may have some cheese stashed away if you need it."

Phil eagerly stepped forward—"Oh boy, yes, I could definitely use some cheese! Any crackers, too?"— but Tai cut him off. He stared at the stranger with wide eyes. "Are you Big Ned?"

The mouse looked surprised. "And how did you know that?"

"We know your son, Neddy," Tai said excitedly. "He told us about you."

"Neddy!" the mouse exclaimed. He pressed forward against the bars. "How is he? Is he all right?"

Rumpus shifted uncomfortably. "The Wildhares got to him. They made him give us up."

Tai was quick to explain: "He didn't have a choice."

Even Phil nodded agreement to that.

"They would have thrown him in here with the rest

of us," Big Ned sighed. He gestured out. "Poor guys. Most of them wouldn't hurt a fly."

Phil snorted, eyeing the toothy fox.

"Really," Big Ned said earnestly. "They're here because they didn't fit in with Mayor Pleasant's standards. Too rough, too wild, too . . . weird."

Phil looked again. Sure, they seemed a little rough, a bit scraggly—but that didn't make them the villains, right? In fact, for all his fancy clothes and manners, Mayor Pleasant was the rottenest person in town.

"Neddy's a good boy," Big Ned said sadly. He looked so small, nothing like they'd expected of the sheriff who took down the Wildhares and stood up to the mayor.

"He'll be all right," Tai assured him. "The mayor needs him at Pleasant Day tomorrow. He's in charge of the hamster races."

"Bah—Pleasant Day," Big Ned scoffed. "Back in my day, it wasn't all about celebrating the badger."

"Neddy said it used to be about art," Rumpus prompted.

Big Ned nodded. Prompted by her reporter's instincts, Phlox took out her notebook and began taking notes as the mouse talked.

"It was Little Neddy's favorite day," Big Ned recalled fondly. "The food was always excellent: Our cooks were artists themselves. Gooseberry pies, fried funnel cakes, kettle-cooked popcorn, and, of course, deep-fried cheese wedges. But most of all, Neddy loved seeing everyone's art."

Phil's stomach rumbled unhappily.

"What kind of art?" Phlox asked, pencil poised.

"Oh, all kinds." Big Ned tipped his head back as he thought. "Some folks worked with metal, some with stone. People traded figurines and glass works. The tribe's work made the biggest splash, of course." He smiled. "When that little owl girl brought in her golden vases, I thought the whole town was going to go crazy."

"Bright Eyes?" Phlox asked, smiling.

"Yep. Chief Talon's daughter," Big Ned said. "No one knows how she got those vases so perfect. And my Neddy was smitten—with the art and the artist."

Out of the corner of his eye, Tai noticed that their jailor had wandered closer. Though he was facing the other way, his long ears were cocked in their direction.

"After that, the two of them were always together—Neddy and Bright Eyes. Whatever she taught him, it stuck. He really started working on his art. He loved to paint the river, and he got pretty good at it. Bright Eyes started collaborating with him and he started putting little bits of gold in his river paintings." Big Ned chuckled. "She convinced him to share a table with her at the festival. When they showed the pieces they'd worked on together, it was all anyone could talk about."

Phlox caught Tai's eye and nodded toward the jailor, who now stood very close and hung on Big Ned's every word. Tai arched his eyebrows at Phlox: Why was the hare so interested? Phlox nodded. A plan was beginning to form.

"This town was famous for art," Big Ned was saying. "The finest pieces were displayed in City Hall—before the Badger replaced them with portraits of himself."

Just then Phlox interrupted with a dramatic cry: "This is all just a big mistake! If only we could explain to the mayor!"

"Yes," Tai said, matching Phlox's sorrowful tone. "We could show him how much we admire his town!"

Rumpus, Phil, and Big Ned stared at Phlox and Tai as if they'd gone crazy. The scrawny jailor cocked his head, clearly confused.

"And to think tomorrow is Pleasant Day," Phlox said. She snapped her fingers: "I know! We should make the mayor a portrait! He'd look . . . majestic. And you three are such accomplished artists."

"Think how generous he'd be," Tai carried on, "to everyone who helped make such a fine gift possible!"

Jack's ears twitched eagerly. "You're artists?"

"Very popular artists," Phlox said. "Their work is everywhere around here!" She winked at her friends.

Phil chuckled, and Rumpus coughed until he could control himself.

"And you want to make a majestic gift for the mayor?" the hare asked.

"We do!" Tai said. He tried to look innocent. "We'd paint him in all his finery—he'd practically be gleaming. In fact, the painting would shimmer like gold."

The Wildhare had a faraway look in his eyes. "Gold . . ." he murmured.

"Mayor Pleasant would be so grateful," Phlox coaxed. "Surely he'd reward anyone who brought him that kind of present." She smiled winningly. "Would you be able to help us? If it isn't too much trouble. You seem like the kind to appreciate art."

"All we need," Tai jumped in, "is the backpack with our art supplies in it. It's right there next to you. We just need the paint inside. And a canvas, of course."

Jack chewed his bottom lip. Finally he nodded. "All right, I'll get your supplies. But no funny business!" He tried to look menacing, but his ears waggled in excitement.

The jailor walked over to the backpack.

"What are you two up to?" Phil demanded.

"We're breaking out of here," Tai whispered. He turned to Big Ned. "Big Ned, we'll need your help. Pass the word. If Phlox is going where I think she's going with this, we're going to need everyone on board . . ."

Jack returned with a canvas and spray cans from the backpack. He looked skeptically at the friends. "You're going to paint with these?"

"They're the finest materials gold can buy," Phlox assured him, with an earnest expression.

The jailor handed them over slowly, not quite convinced. "What kind of portrait are you doing again?" he asked.

Rumpus started shaking the cans. The hare backed away nervously at the sound.

"We're going to paint the mayor's victory against the tribe," Tai said. "It'll be a tribute to the mayor's success—thanks to the brave and daring Wildhares, of course."

The jailor hooked his thumbs in his suspenders, looking proud. "Of course," he said.

"It would be great to have someone pose for the portrait," Rumpus said as he set up the canvas. "The mayor will be front and center, of course, but if we had someone to stand in for the Wildhares . . ."

"You'll paint me in it," Jack said sharply. He tried to snarl, but his ears gave away his eagerness. "After all, I'll also be the one to deliver it to Mayor Pleasant."

"What a great idea!" Phil exclaimed. "We'll paint you at the head of the charge, running off those cowardly war hawks as the mayor stands triumphant."

The jailor's eyes gleamed.

"That's a great idea," Rumpus told the jailor. "Why don't you try a few poses and let's see what would work."

The hare stood at attention with his hand at his forehead in a salute.

Rumpus coughed. "Something . . . a bit more casual."

The jailor slumped against the wall, cocking his hip and smiling lazily.

"Maybe a little more energetic," Phlox prompted. "Imagine: You're chasing down a band of war hawks. The mayor is counting on you!"

The Wildhare obligingly struck a running pose, arms outstretched, grinning wildly.

"Perfect!" Rumpus said. "If you could just move a little to your left."

Jack hopped to the left.

"A little more."

He did. Silently, in the shadows behind him, the gecko with the hard stare in the neighboring cell

reached between the bars and plucked the keys from the Wildhare's belt with his suction-cup fingers.

"Bingo!" Phil shouted, startling everyone. He smiled apologetically.

Rumpus continued to direct the hare into all sorts of poses: leaping, fighting, charging, crouching. Meanwhile, the keys were quietly passed from cell to cell.

"Good, good." Rumpus kept spraying—*pssht pssht*—to cover up the sound of cell locks clicking open. "We've just about got it."

Finally, he gestured with a big smile. "Would you like to see? I think Mayor Pleasant will love this."

The jailor came forward excitedly. When Rumpus flipped the painting around, Jack's ears sprang up in shock. "What's that supposed to be?" he asked, pointing at the random squiggles.

Phil laughed. "A distraction."

Slowly, the Wildhare turned around. The prisoners stood outside their cells, watching in amusement.

"Now," Big Ned drawled, "we can do this the easy way, or the hard way."

Jack was no trouble after that. The prisoners tied him up in one of the cells and locked the door gleefully behind them.

It was nearing dusk, and gaslights started to flicker on all over town. One by one, the prisoners crept out of the jailhouse and gathered behind a barn.

"Thank you for your help," Big Ned told the four friends. "We can distract the Wildhares while you sneak out of town. We're staying here to take down the mayor once and for all." His fellow prisoners nodded in agreement.

Tai looked around. "But . . . there's a whole horde out there," he said. "You're vastly outnumbered."

Big Ned looked very fierce for someone so small. "That may be true, but we have to try. We made this town back in the day, and we're willing to fight to get it back."

Rumpus straightened. "Give us a moment, Big Ned." He led his friends aside, and they conferred among one another.

"Who knows how we got here, but in a weird way, this is our town, too," said Rumpus. "We should help set things right."

Tai smiled. "Let's do it for Neddy!"

"Hear, hear!" Phlox cheered. "And for the tribe!"

"What?" Phil exclaimed. "Aren't they the ones who tried to shoot us?"

"Bright Eyes helped me see their side," Phlox explained passionately. "They're only trying to protect their home from the Badger."

"But what about us?" Phil said. "Why are we helping everyone else when we don't even know how we got here or how to find our way home? Shouldn't we be figuring that out?"

A grin flashed on Phlox's face. "Oh yeah! We've been so busy running I haven't had a chance to tell you guys. Grandmother Buffalo has the answers—I've seen them."

"Seen them?" Tai asked.

"What makes you so sure about this Grandmother Buffalo?" Rumpus grumbled. "Especially when we'd have to dodge war hawks again just to get back to her."

Phlox straightened her glasses. "We're hardly safer in town, with the Wildhares. If we go to the caves we can get answers from Grandmother Buffalo and ask the war hawks to help Big Ned!"

"Do you really think Chief Talon would help?" asked Tai.

"It's worth a shot," Phlox said. "He and Big Ned used to be friends. And these guys are no match for the Wildhares on their own, no matter how brave."

The four friends walked back to Big Ned. "We're going to the Claw Foot Tribe," Rumpus said. "We're going to ask them to help you."

Big Ned raised his eyebrows. "Chief Talon is awful prickly," he warned. "He's not one to change his mind easily."

"We have a secret weapon." Phlox grinned. "Bright Eyes."

Big Ned laughed. "Well, maybe then you'll have a chance. We'll hole up here and wait for you."

"See you soon, Big Ned." Rumpus shook his hand. "We'll be back as soon as we can."

Neddy sat by the river, his gold pan next to him. He'd tried all evening to figure out a plan to go back to town and save his friends, but so far he'd come up with nothing. One mouse against a whole squad of Wildhares — what chance did he have?

Panning helped him think. He liked to watch the water slosh and swirl around the black dirt, and it usually thrilled him to catch a flicker of something shiny in the dull pan. But tonight all he could do was stare guiltily at the stars on the horizon.

He heard something: people approaching. He jumped up in fear. What if the Wildhares were here to snatch him again? Was there time to hide in the bushes? But then he thought of Tai, and of his father, and straightened as tall as he could to face the approaching party.

"Neddy!"

Shocked, the little mouse could only stare in bewilderment as Tai bounded toward him. Rumpus and Phil were hot on his heels, followed by Phlox.

"W-what are you doing here?" Neddy asked unsteadily. A smile started to spread across his features. "Why aren't you in jail?"

Phil waved his hand. "We didn't really like the service there. I don't recommend it."

"We're glad you're OK, Neddy," Rumpus said. "We wanted to make sure the Wildhares hadn't done any worse to you once they hauled us away."

Neddy looked down at the ground in shame. "I'm sorry about that."

Tai patted his friend's shoulder. "You did what you had to do," he said. Then he smiled. "Besides, it worked out for the best. We broke your dad out of jail, too."

Neddy stared at the four friends with awe. "Really? He's free?"

"He's a good man," Rumpus nodded. "He stayed in town to take down the mayor tomorrow at the Pleasant Day celebration."

"And we're headed to see Bright Eyes and Grandmother Buffalo," said Phlox, "and to convince Chief Talon to help your dad." She winked. "If you wanted to tag along . . . ?"

Neddy blushed.

"Of course I'll go," Neddy said with growing confidence. "It's high time the mayor and the Wildhares get what's coming to them."

"That's the spirit!" Phil said.

"Welcome to Talking Rock Caves!" Phlox said with a flourish. Huge stalactites hung from the ceiling and dripped into little pools. It was quiet and cool—a welcome change from the hot desert they'd ridden through.

"This is incredible!" Tai said. He leaned over one of the pools. Deep in the water, Tai could see the bright shine of gold.

"You haven't seen anything yet," Phlox said.

She led them deeper into the network of caves and into a larger chamber, which was lit by torches.

One long, high stone wall was as perfectly smooth as a canvas. As they walked closer, they saw that it was indeed covered in paintings.

"Oh, wow!" Rumpus breathed.

So many colors! So many designs! The fantastic mural stretched on and on, vivid scene after vivid scene. Phlox ran forward, pointing to one scene.

"See this?" she said excitedly. "This is the Golden Sky Dance." The painting showed war hawks twisting gracefully in the sky, feathers outstretched.

"They celebrate it every year. It's one of Bright Eyes's favorite festivals," Phlox explained. "And this one . . ." She pointed to a picture of houses carved into the side of a cliff. "This is their home. They call it the Roost. It's taken hundreds of years to carve out the caves. And this one . . ." She explained scene after scene, each more colorful than the last. The paintings told the history of the Claw Foot Tribe, and tales of their heroes: great Chief Thunderbird who brought peace to the warring tribes; quick and nimble Lightfeather, who could dodge rattle-can snakes with ease; and sneaky Gray Crow, the trickster thief.

Phlox walked to the middle of the mural and pointed. "And this is where our story begins."

Tai walked closer, transfixed. There they were: a rhino, tiger, and two prairie dogs chased by a herd of cattlefish; the three boys walking through town; and riding their hamsters across the desert.

"How could anyone have painted this?" Tai asked. "These things just happened."

"It was on this wall long before you ever came to our land," said a gentle voice behind them.

They spun around. Bright Eyes was smiling at them, and next to her was an old buffalo woman, kindly smiling as well.

"Grandmother Buffalo," Phlox said. "This is Tai, Rumpus, and my brother, Phil. Guys, this is Grandmother Buffalo."

"What you see has been there for a thousand years," Grandmother Buffalo said. "It's our story. And you're a part of it. Ah, look . . ."

They turned to the wall and, as they watched, a square of mural suddenly flashed. Startled, the boys leapt back.

The flash quickly died. But the scene, originally the same dark colors as the rest of the mural, was now brightly colored and shining with light. It showed a rhino, two prairie dogs, a tiger, a buffalo, and a little owl staring at a painted wall.

"But that's us," Phil said numbly. "Right now."

"It's the strange paint that Grandpa Horn gave us," Tai whispered. He reached out as if to touch the wall but pulled his hand back at the last second. "It glittered the same way."

"The scenes light up as things happen," Bright Eyes said. "They glow for a while. Eventually, they return to normal, but we always remember those shining moments."

"This is history and prophecy," Phlox said. "What happened, what's going to happen—it's all here."

Phil noticed something and leaned forward. When he realized what it was, he groaned. "Really?" he asked, throwing his hands in the air. "Of all the moments to have been mysteriously painted on the wall, that has to be one of them?" The scene showed three figures crashed to the ground, drenched in paint, as hamsters galloped away. Grinning, Phlox took out her camera and snapped the scene. Phil glared at her. "What?" She shrugged. "I have to get the whole story."

"Guys, look at this," Rumpus said, directing their attention to a scene farther down. It was big, bigger than the ones around it. On the left a group of townspeople; on the right, a flock of war hawk braves. They faced off, looking like they were going to collide.

"That doesn't look so good," Rumpus murmured.

"But look," Tai said. He pointed to the town side, where two small figures led the charge. "Could that be Neddy and his father?"

Phil squinted. "Maybe. And that," he pointed toward a dark, menacing bird, "is definitely Chief Talon."

"That hasn't happened yet," Bright Eyes said. "It's part of the prophecy."

"And the paintings aren't always as they seem," Grandmother Buffalo explained. "Some are clear only after the events occur."

Everyone fell silent—someone was approaching. It was Neddy, who had been feeding and watering their

hamsters outside the cave. At the sight of Bright Eyes, his face lit up. Bright Eyes broke into a wide grin, and the two friends ran to each other. Bright Eyes twirled the small mouse around as he laughed. Then they huddled in their own little world, catching up.

"I must show you something," said Grandmother Buffalo. Stepping carefully on the uneven rocks, she led the friends to the wall's far end, to the first scene. "This is not the first time you've appeared on our wall."

Phlox and the boys stared in wonder. This scene was painted in a very different style, with random squiggles throughout. It was harder to tell what was going on in it. But there they were: what could only be a group of four young artists. Behind them was the painting they were working on: a desert landscape.

"Chief Talon would not believe me," Grandmother Buffalo said, "but I think you are the First Scribblers, who drew color and action to our world. Who started our first story and are destined to set things right."

Tai's mouth dropped open, and Phil raised his eyebrows. "So we're, like, gods or something?" he asked.

Rumpus scowled at him, but Grandmother Buffalo chuckled. "Oh, not quite. More like . . . guardians of fate who had a beautiful dream." She looked down the wall, where a badger gripped handfuls of gold. "A dream now threatened by greed and pride."

The young artists looked guiltily at one another, remembering how they had argued over the mural, fighting for every inch of painting surface and wanting to outdo the others. None of them had painted the badger. But he clearly reflected their own greed and pride, and unwillingness to collaborate and work together.

Grandmother Buffalo swayed. In an instant, Bright Eyes was there, offering her arm. "Grandmother," the owl said, "you must rest. I'll help you back to your cave, and return for our visitors."

Grandmother Buffalo gave the group one last smile. "I'm so glad to have met you, after seeing your story for so many years. Please visit me again, when this rotten business with the badger is finally settled."

"We will!" the friends promised.

As Grandmother Buffalo and Bright Eyes disappeared into one of the tunnels, Neddy and the friends continued studying the mural.

"It's amazing, isn't it?" Neddy said. "I have to say, I didn't quite believe it when Bright Eyes told me the story. But seeing you guys here . . ."

"It's definitely something," Rumpus chuffed.

"A little intimidating," said Tai.

"Absolutely awesome," Phil exclaimed. "Think about it—we're part of the prophecy! Our story has been magically painted on this wall for hundreds of years! Isn't that wild?"

"It's a big responsibility," Rumpus said, straightening up. "We have to stop the mayor and save the town. That's going to be quite a challenge."

Phil waved him off. "No prob. We just convinced the mayor we were millionaires, broke out of jail, and learned we were destined to save the world." He smirked. "Anything else is a piece of cake!"

As soon as the words left his mouth, a fierce, shrill battle cry echoed through the chamber.

"You just had to say it, didn't you?" Rumpus muttered.

Chief Talon's headdress stood tall on his head, exaggerating his already fearsome appearance. Phlox tried to remember that he was Bright Eyes's father, but somehow this did little to make him less frightening. Standing in the mouth of the cavern, Chief Talon blocked their exit, and war hawks emerged from all the other tunnels that led deeper into the mountain. The five friends were surrounded.

"Enemies in our Talking Rock Caves," said Chief Talon angrily. "Get them out of here immediately."

Five war hawks advanced and tied up the friends.

"Take them to the holding area," said Chief Talon. "Diver, Lightning, do not let them out of your sight." They nodded. "I need to find my daughter. She must answer for this intrusion." With a fierce toss of his head, Chief Talon left the friends to their captors.

They were led out of the cave and along the steep ledge of the cliff, winding downward. The desert wind had picked up and threatened to sweep them off the edge. Phlox was almost glad to have a powerful war hawk hanging on to her. Finally they reached another cave entrance. The opening was small and hidden—invisible to those who didn't know it was there.

"Inside," said Diver gruffly. He nudged the friends forward and they obediently filed into a dark, cool tunnel that led finally to a large chamber. Diver lit a torch and the room turned orange with its glow. The shadows of the friends and the war hawks stretched eerily along the cavern walls. Tai shivered. Battle scenes covered the walls of the chamber—meant to intimidate prisoners, Tai thought.

"Lightning and I will take it from here," Diver told the other war hawks. "Dismissed."

The other three war hawks disappeared back down the tunnel. As far as Tai could tell, the tunnel was the only way in or out, unless there was a secret door hidden somewhere. He felt uneasy, but he hoped what Bright Eyes said was true: The war hawks were honorable. They wouldn't hurt their captives or lock them up forever. Would they?

"Stand against the wall," said Lightning.

The five friends lined up and Diver and Lightning searched their pockets. In Phil's pockets they found two paintbrushes and the small gold piece the ground sloth had given him as a tip back at the train station. Tai had only a compass, and from Phlox the war hawks took her pencil and notebook. Neddy's button-size pockets contained a tiny block of cheese and a sheriff's badge. "That was my dad's badge," Neddy said. "I carry it for luck."

Lightning pulled a can of spray paint from Rumpus's backpack. The rattle from the can startled him. He dropped the can and it rolled toward Diver.

"A rattle-can snake!" Diver yelped, jumping back from it.

The spray can came to a stop and made no more noise. Diver reached down to pick it up. "Is it an infant rattle-can snake? Is it dead?"

"It's not a snake," said Rumpus. "It's paint."

"Paint?" said Lightning doubtfully.

"We use them to paint cool murals," boasted Phil. Then he faltered, remembering how they had gotten into the predicament they were in that very minute.

"Go ahead," said Rumpus. "Try the paint."

Diver pointed the can at the wall and let out a couple spurts of blue. He reached out to touch the paint.

"Careful! It could be poisonous," warned Lightning.

"If it was rattle-can snake venom," said Diver, "it would burn a hole through the wall. That is what the legends say."

The war hawks stared at the blue spot. When nothing happened, Diver said, "Huh, I guess it *is* paint."

Just then, without a sound, Chief Talon appeared, surprising everyone, even Lightning and Diver. To the five friends' disappointment, he was alone, without his daughter. He folded his wings behind his back and addressed his captives. "Bright Eyes claims you have come in peace," said Chief Talon. "And yet I see you have come armed." He gestured toward the spray cans from Rumpus's backpack lined up along the ground. "That was not wise."

"Actually, Chief," said Diver. "These aren't dangerous. They're just cans of paint." He picked up another can and spray-painted an artrow on the wall.

"Hey! That's pretty good," said Phil.

"Quiet!" Chief Talon snapped. He looked closely at Diver's artrow but shook his head dismissively. "No matter. These five are still trespassers, thieves, and allies of the Badger. Now that they've seen the Talking Rock Caves, we cannot let them go free. There's no telling what they've already told our enemy."

"We didn't tell the badger anything," said Rumpus. "But he told us plenty."

"Yeah," chimed in Phil, "he told us all about his plans to take over your territory."

"The Badger take over my land?" scoffed Chief

Talon. "Impossible. Not with my war hawks ready to defend it!" He began pacing back and forth.

"Chief Talon," said Tai. "We came to warn you about the badger, but we're also here to ask for help."

"Those townspeople have been trespassing and stealing my gold for years," argued Chief Talon. "Why should I help them?"

"They were forced to by the mayor," said Tai. "They don't like him either. But they had no choice. He threatened to throw them in prison, like he did to Big Ned."

"Buck Wildhare is rounding up every Wildhare brother, cousin, and uncle he has for Pleasant Day," said Rumpus. "There could be hundreds of them."

"My dad is out of jail now, and tomorrow he's leading the townspeople against the mayor and Buck," said Neddy. His small voice quavered as it echoed around the chamber. "He always said you were a great chief—noble and brave. He said you were an even better friend." Neddy looked at the chief with his large shining eyes. "My dad could sure use a friend right now."

Chief Talon's face softened. "Your father must be very proud of you, Neddy," he said. The chief sighed. "Go tell your father his friend will not let him down."

The cavern erupted in cheers from Rumpus, Tai,

Phil, Phlox, and Neddy. The glow of the torch now seemed warm and friendly and the cavern full of hope.

"Lightning, Diver, gather all the war hawks," said Chief Talon. "We'll meet at Artrow Bluff when the sun sets tonight."

"Our arrival at Pleasant Day must be a surprise," the chief told the five friends. "We'll need to coordinate with Big Ned."

"I'll go let him know," said Neddy.

"You'll make a fine sheriff one day," said Chief Talon. He followed his warriors down the tunnel.

"We're all coming with you," Rumpus told Neddy.

"Yeah, no way you're fighting all those Wildhares without us," said Phil.

Neddy looked at his friends gratefully. "How can I ever repay you?"

"You're our friend," said Tai. "That's all there is to it."

"Leaving already?" It was Bright Eyes, entering the chamber.

"Bright Eyes, where have you been?" exclaimed Phlox. "Are you OK? We were worried."

"I was grounded for a while," said Bright Eyes. "But I knew my father would come around about your mission."

"I think we're still missing something important we're supposed to learn from the prophecies," Phlox said to Bright Eyes. "I'd like to see if I can make any more sense of the cavern paintings."

"I'd like to study them more as well," said Tai. "If it's all right with Bright Eyes for us to be here, that is."

"I have the same feeling," agreed Bright Eyes. "I'll stay with you two."

"We'll plan to meet the rest of you outside town later tonight," said Phlox. "Good luck, you guys."

"You, too," returned Rumpus.

"The rest of us better get going," said Neddy. "Pleasant Day starts first thing in the morning. Once we find out my dad's strategy, I'll send a smoke signal."

"Don't forget this," said Bright Eyes, picking up the sheriff's badge and pinning it to Neddy's overalls. Then she gave him a kiss on the cheek, and the little mouse turned pink all the way to the tips of his ears.

Phlox, Tai, and Bright Eyes watched anxiously as their friends jumped onto their hamster mounts and began their trek back across the desert.

The mountains of the Claw Foot Tribe were busy with movement. War hawks circled overhead, planning the route to Pleasant Junction. In a large cave near Artrow Bluff, artrows were being made by the hundreds. Phlox, Tai, and Bright Eyes helped restring and polish the war hawks' bows.

"Do you think the war hawks can really defeat the mayor and all those Wildhares?" asked Tai. "What if the badger has something up his sleeve? Some dirty trick the war hawks aren't prepared for?"

"I wish I knew what we should do." Phlox sighed. "The prophecy says four strangers are supposed to reunite this land, but it doesn't say how."

"Come on," said Tai. "We need another look at Talking Rock."

Bright Eyes, Phlox, and Tai made their way up the steep bluffs and down the tunnels to the cavern. They settled in front of the paintings and stared hard. "There must be something we've missed," said Phlox.

"So far all the paintings have come true," said Tai. He traced over the cattlefish, the war hawks, the badger. "Everything but these last two panels. But I can't make out what they mean."

"Bright Eyes," said Phlox, "what are these squiggly lines? Are they a symbol for something?" She pointed to the wavy lines scattered through the paintings.

"Those represent the rattle-can snakes," said Bright Eyes. As soon as she said the name, the wavy lines started to squirm. They lit up for a moment before turning dull and still again.

"Did you see that?" Tai asked, eyes wide.

"The rattle-can snakes are mysterious creatures that wander the desert, belonging to no tribe or town," Bright Eyes explained. "We know little about them except that they possess great power. Their venom is highly poisonous and their metallic scales almost indestructible."

"Sounds like a perfect weapon in battle," said Tai. "Maybe they could help us."

"They do not fight in battles," said Bright Eyes. "They are too wise for that. And besides, you would never find one. They're only found when they want to be found."

"How about these?" said Phlox, studying the last couple of paintings. "That's the City Hall at Pleasant Junction. But what are we supposed to do there?"

"When in doubt, go with your strengths," said Bright Eyes. "That's what Grandmother Buffalo always says."

"Our strengths," said Tai thoughtfully. "You don't have any extra paint around here, do you?"

Rumpus, Phil, and Neddy made good time back across the desert toward Pleasant Junction. Without being chased by war hawks or Wildhares, the ride was rather smooth.

"There's home," said Neddy. Ahead was the dark outline of buildings. By the time they reached the edge of town, loud shouting and laughter could be heard—unusual for such a normally quiet place.

"What's all that noise?" whispered Rumpus.

"Sounds like a party," said Phil.

Then came the *BOOM* of the battlebee cannon. Laughter turned to angry shouts.

"Mongo, you idiot!"

"Not again!"

"Mongo did uh oh."

Rumpus, Phil, and Neddy dismounted and crept on foot into the town center. Right in front of City Hall was a huge blazing bonfire and what looked like hundreds of hares running wild.

"Looks like all Buck's Wildhare relatives have arrived," said Neddy. "Come on, we need to find my dad and the others."

"The stables and your campsite are probably being watched," said Rumpus. "Where could your dad be hiding?"

"There's only one other place my dad would go," said Neddy. "Follow me."

On the other side of the train tracks, a gigantic formation of boulders was surrounded by cactuses. Neddy slipped easily between two of the prickly plants, but the opening was too small even for Phil.

"Neddy!" Rumpus hissed. "Wait up, we can't fit!"

Neddy popped his head back out. "Oh, right, sorry!" He disappeared again. Rumpus and Phil heard three knocks, and then one of the cactuses swung open on hinges. "Trick cactus," said Neddy, holding the door open as Rumpus and Phil walked uncertainly through.

They followed Neddy into a surprisingly spacious clearing sheltered all around by tall boulders. There were Big Ned and dozens of townspeople, quietly making plans.

"Neddy!" Big Ned exclaimed. "My boy! You're safe!" Father and son embraced. "And you've brought our jail breakers!"

"At your service, Sheriff," said Phil with a salute.

"Anything we can do to help," added Rumpus.

"That's mighty noble of you," said Big Ned. "But this is going to be a dangerous, one-sided battle. We didn't expect so many Wildhares to show up and I wouldn't be surprised if more arrive tomorrow."

"We saw," said Phil.

"So, boys," Big Ned concluded, wiping his brow, "I sure appreciate your bravery, but I can't let you fight."

"But we want to help," said Rumpus. "We care about this town, and we want to help save it."

"Besides," said Phil, "we have a secret weapon."

"You do?" Big Ned said, perking up.

"We sure do, Dad," said Neddy happily. "And Chief Talon said to tell you your friend won't let you down."

"Talon? My friend?" said Big Ned in wonder. "The chief is going to help us?"

"His war hawks, too," said Rumpus.

"They're gathering as we speak," said Neddy. "Just waiting for our signal."

"Well, that changes things!" Big Ned perked up. "We have a chance with the war hawks on our side. A darn good one!"

Big Ned and Neddy did a little jig in celebration, spinning and wheeling around Rumpus and Phil.

Phlox and Tai set off that night for Pleasant Junction. Tai had a big burlap sack tied to his hamster saddle and his compass in hand. The desert stretched for miles. Cacti dotted the horizon here and there, and the star-studded sky seemed to go on forever.

"If we keep heading straight we should get there in just a couple of hours," said Tai.

"I can't wait to tell the others our plan," said Phlox. "Tomorrow is going to be a day nobody will forget!"

Tai was about to chime in, but he paused and rotated his ears around. "Did you hear that?" They slowed their hamsters. "It sounded like some kind of howl."

"Well," said Phlox, "the desert is full of wild animals . . ."

They rode in silence, listening to the eerie sounds of the desert: chirps and calls of all kinds, and the whipping of the wind.

"There it is again!" Tai said.

"I hear it, too," said Phlox, frightened. "It must be getting closer. But it doesn't sound like a howl so much as a . . . shriek."

"I read that coyotes' calls sound like screams," said Tai. "I'm starting to wish we had asked a war hawk to come with us. Let's ride faster."

They urged their hamsters to a gallop. Tai's sensitive ears twitched. "That's strange . . . I hear rustling sounds, like grass, but out here there's only sand." He turned around in his saddle. Several tumbleweeds were blowing behind them, rolling and skittering over the ground.

"Even the tumbleweeds are creepy out here," said Tai.

"Yeah," Phlox laughed nervously.

Suddenly the tumbleweeds picked up speed, rolling faster than the wind could possibly have been carrying them.

"What the . . . ?" said Phlox.

As the massave grass balls rolled nearer, huge mouths opened wide to reveal long, pointy teeth.

"Yikes!" Tai yelled.

With terrifying, high-pitched shrieks, the tumbleweeds lunged, snapping their sharp fangs.

"Tai!" Phlox shouted. "What do we do??"

"I'm thinking! I'm thinking!"

"If we make it out of this craziness, Rumpus
is getting an earful!" yelled Phlox. "Him
and his bizarre imagination!"

Then they heard a familiar rattle. The tumbleweeds heard it, too, because they immediately let the wind whisk them away. Barely believing their luck, Tai and Phlox slowed their hamsters. Tai slid down from his hamster, legs shaking. He spotted something silver slithering away.

"Hey, wait!" Tai shouted. He ran after the rattle-can snake, Phlox on his heels. "We want to thank you!"

The rattle-can snake did not stop, but turned its head toward Tai and Phlox and said, "You had besssst be on your way."

Its voice made Tai and Phlox shiver, but they charged on, determined. "Please! Stop!" Phlox yelled.

The rattle-can snake halted. "How curioussss," it said. "No one ever chassssses ussssss. They alwayssss run away."

Tai and Phlox walked closer to the mysterious creature—definitely within striking range. Its metallic skin shone in the moonlight, and its purple eyes sparkled.

"S-sorry to bother you," said Tai. "We just . . ."

". . . want to say thanks for helping us," Phlox said. "I thought we were done for."

"We appear where we are needed," said the rattle-can snake. "That issssss all."

"Well then, I hate to ask for another favor," Phlox

said, "but we have a desperate situation. You are needed tomorrow in Pleasant Junction."

"Oh yessss," said the rattle-can snake. "I know all about tomorrow'sssss battle."

"Oh great!" said Tai. "So can you help us?"

"But we do not choose ssssides," it said. "We sssssupport neither the mayor nor the tribe againsssst each other. Our conccccccern goessss beyond their sssssquabble."

"But the badger and Buck Wildhare have done terrible things!" Tai protested. "They're the bad guys! Something has to be done."

"Then do ssssssomething," said the snake.

"Us?? But we don't know how!" cried Phlox.

"I'd get back on your hamstersss if I were you. There are more dangerous things than tumbleweeds out here," the snake warned and started to slither away.

"Are you going to help us?" Tai shouted after it.

"The work issssn't finished until it glowssssss. Only then can you sssssee all the piecessssss. In time help will be given."

And the rattle-can snake was out of sight.

"Here they come!" Rumpus whispered.

Hiding behind a building, Rumpus, Phil and Neddy watched the two shadows creep closer. One was small and low to the ground, moving quickly, while the larger shape bounded nimbly, a sack over its shoulder. Rumpus leaned out and hissed, "Over here!"

Tai and Phlox arrived breathless.

"So what's the plan?" Rumpus asked.

Tai smiled. "We just have to get to City Hall. The only problem is the Wildhares between here and there."

Neddy rubbed his hands together. "You let me take care of those brutes. I'll meet you at City Hall."

Tai looked worried. "You sure, Neddy?"

There was an excitement in the mouse's smile that made him look a lot like his fierce and courageous father, Big Ned. "I've got this!" he promised.

Neddy scampered off, and the four friends snuck down alleys until they reached the big, white marble City Hall. In front, three Wildhares stood guarding a very big burlap-wrapped something. Whatever was inside, it was easily over ten feet tall. Phil tried to move closer to see, but Tai pulled him back. "Not yet," Tai whispered. "Too many of them."

"While we're waiting, fill us in on the plan, guys," Rumpus urged.

Phlox pointed to the vast side wall of City Hall—painted with yet another billboard of Mayor Pleasant and his greedy grin. "We think that needs redecorating."

Tai opened his sack, revealing the paints and brushes he and Phlox had collected from Talking Rock Caves. "How about replacing that badger with a mural that inspires the town and reminds them who they really are?"

"Let's get to work!" Rumpus said, unzipping his backpack and pulling out spray paint cans.

Suddenly, there was a commotion in front of City Hall. A Wildhare ran up to the guards, gesturing crazily and hopping. Then all the hares dashed away, hooting.

"Wow," Tai said, impressed. "Neddy delivered."

"Come on," Rumpus whispered. "Let's get started."

Even in the dead of night, with only the bright moon and weak gas lamps for light, the four of them had the time of their lives making the mural. Phlox directed them, pointing out spots here or there that needed particular touches from one artist or another,

and sketching scenes with a brush for Tai to fill in with his spray paint. Phil darted between Rumpus's legs and jumped up onto Tai's shoulders to reach low and high areas.

"That looks fantastic, scribblers!" Neddy said, arriving just as they were adding the final touches.

Tai turned with a grin. "Neddy!" he exclaimed. "How did you get the Wildhare guards to scatter?"

Neddy smirked cheekily. "Oh, some bits of gold may have been discovered strategically planted just outside town. . . . And nobody comes between a Wildhare and his gold!"

"You started a fake gold rush?" Phil chuckled. "That's brilliant!"

"While they're busy doing that, let's get to sleep. We have a big day tomorrow," said Rumpus.

"Wait just a second," Tai said. He pulled a big sheet out of his sack and he and Rumpus secured it over the mural so it was hidden from sight.

They all started for the stables, but as they passed the large burlap-covered object in front of the City Hall, Phlox's curiosity kicked into gear. While Tai was telling the others about the tumbleweeds and the rattle-can snake's strange promises, Phlox slowly lifted a corner of the burlap.

Her eyebrows shot up at the sight of a bright yellow glimmer. She kept pulling, and pulling, until the burlap cover fell to the ground and the object was fully revealed. The boys turned and gasped.

A humongous, larger-than-life statue of the mayor stood before them. A giant golden statue. One arm

pointed toward the west, to the gold-rich Claw Foot territory that the mayor hoped would soon be his.

"That no good, rotten . . ." Neddy trailed off, fuming. "This is why he wanted all that gold?! To think: Those fines were going toward a big statue of himself!"

"The ego on this guy," Phil muttered, agreeing.

Phlox rolled her eyes. "He certainly has a high opinion of himself," she said, kicking the statue.

A slow grin spread over Phil's face. He picked up a paint brush. "Rumpus, give me a lift!"

The rhino smiled. "I like the way you think."

With rodent nimbleness and artful flair, Phil clambered all over the statue, painting an eye patch, smudges, and other special touches. His friends dissolved in giggles with each addition. Finally, Phil dropped to the ground, dusting off his hands with satisfaction.

Just then, Tai's sensitive feline ears picked up a sound. "Company coming! Rumpus, cover the statue!"

The friends crept into the shadows and held their breath as the Wildhares resumed their places in front of City Hall. No one noticed the lopsided burlap over the statue or the sheet covering the billboard.

"See you hares in the morning!" Rumpus whispered.

Pleasant Day was bright and warm. The townspeople gathered in the square around City Hall, nearly silent, shifting nervously. Despite the quickly building heat, many wore long coats or capes, with strange lumps underneath.

At last, the mayor made his grand entrance out of City Hall. Grinning triumphantly at the large crowd, he descended the white marble steps.

From under the brim of his large hat, Tai looked around. Big Ned and his men were supposed to be here, too, but it was hard to tell who was who in the crush of people. That was good, he supposed. Neddy had disappeared into the crowd as well, trying to get closer to City Hall to do his part.

Meanwhile, Phlox kept her eyes peeled for Bright Eyes and the war hawks: any speck on the horizon, any flash of feathers in the sky. When a Wildhare stepped into her line of sight, she quickly looked away.

"My beloved town," Mayor Pleasant boomed. "Welcome to this year's Pleasant Day festival, celebrating everything that is good and right in this town: order, cleanliness, and prosperity!"

He paused, obviously waiting for applause. The crowd was silent.

Mayor Pleasant cleared his throat, eyeing Buck Wildhare meaningfully. The sheriff smirked and pulled out his snake whip.

A few halfhearted claps filtered through the crowd.

"We're not only celebrating how far we've come from the wild, weird, dirty town this once was," the mayor said. "We're here to dedicate ourselves to a new vision of the future!" He gestured to two Wildhares, who carried the enormous white model town showing the planned expansion. The townspeople, again, were silent.

"And now," the mayor continued, "for the real treat: a memorial to our shining and civilized city!"

Rumpus stood taller, Tai gripped his gear under his poncho, Phil hopped from foot to foot, and Phlox tore her gaze from the sky.

"Sheriff Buck, would you do the honors?" the mayor commanded.

Buck gestured in turn to his brothers. "Spratt, Mongo!"

The brothers stood on either side of the statue and grabbed the burlap. Every time Mongo tugged, Spratt tugged in the opposite direction, getting them absolutely nowhere. "They're not really thinking this through," Tai said wryly.

The crowd was giggling. Finally, Mongo gave a huge tug, lifting Spratt clear off the ground. "Put me down, you oaf!" Spratt squawked.

Mongo blinked. "Oops. Mongo sorry." And with that, he let go of the burlap entirely, releasing both Spratt and the burlap to the ground in a heap . . . and revealing the gigantic golden statue, as well as Phil's handiwork.

The crowd went dead silent, staring in shock. Phlox gave her brother a thumbs-up of congratulations as Mayor Pleasant's face darkened with rage.

"Who did this to me?!" the mayor screeched. "I mean to our town?! Which ruffians are responsible?! Someone fess up right now, or I'll tear down this town— every brick and lamppost. Who? Who?!"

"Here goes," Phil murmured. From under his coat he pulled out a paintbrush and raised it above his head.

Of course, as short as he was, nobody could see it in the crowd.

Rumpus produced a can of spray paint from under his poncho and raised it high into the air.

The mayor saw it immediately. "There he is! Seize him! Seize him!"

Buck's Wildhares started toward Rumpus, but they were slowed by the crowd, which wedged in tighter to block their progress.

Squaring his shoulders, Tai, too, raised his paintbrush. Beside him, Phlox raised her pencil as high as she could.

"Another!" mayor Pleasant shouted. "More villains. Get them! Throw them in jail!"

Then, at the far edge of the square, someone else raised a paintbrush . . . and a painting of a fox family. It was the tooth-picking fox who had been in jail with Big Ned. Beside him, a newt, another recently freed "unpleasant" prisoner, held up a wood sculpture and a chiseling tool.

The mayor swiveled, glaring. "Another, and another! I want all of them brought to . . . justice . . ." He stammered to a halt as he took in the crowd.

All around, on every side, townspeople were raising the artwork and art supplies they'd snuck under their sweaters and capes: paintings, palettes, pottery, clay tools, knitting needles, paintbrushes, embroidery projects, beadwork. Almost every person held up some piece of his or her artwork or art equipment, even children, who waved crayons and marker drawings.

"What is the meaning of this?!" the mayor cried in vexation.

"Now!" boomed Rumpus.

Neddy ripped the sheet off the giant billboard on the side of City Hall. The crowd gasped. Even the mayor looked stunned.

There was no trace of the mayor's grinning face.

Instead, the town gleamed in the sun—the town as it used to be. The shops and houses were painted dozens of assorted colors—bright and wild. Designs decorated every wall, door, and window. And in the mural's center, townsfolk and tribe members happily mingled and admired each other's artwork.

"It really is a good-looking mural," Rumpus said.

"Agreed," said Tai. "We did a great job—together."

"This . . . this is . . ." The mayor was so furious he couldn't speak. All that was missing was a puff of steam rising from his furious head.

"This is the end of the line, mayor."

The crowd parted, revealing a small figure standing in front of the giant statue: Big Ned.

Phil and Tai high-fived each other. "Talk about perfect timing," Phil said.

"You!" The mayor shot an accusing finger at the field mouse. "You are a convict! A menace. This is my town!" he screeched. "You will do as I say!"

"This ain't your town anymore," Big Ned said slowly. "I stand for the law here: always have, always will, no matter who you pay to do your dirty work."

The mayor let out a vicious, angry snarl. He looked like he was going to choke the small mouse.

Swishhh! Out of nowhere, an artrow whistled through the air, striking the golden statue of the mayor right in the forehead.

"Like you said," Tai told Phil, "talk about perfect timing."

"Look, there's Bright Eyes!" Phlox cried, pointing and jumping up and down in excitement.

War hawks swooped in with triumphant screeches, heading right for the Wildhare Gang. Hares scattered every which way out of the square, chased by the war hawk braves. In no time, only the three original Wildhare brothers still stood with Mayor Pleasant.

Bright Eyes landed behind the mayor. Neddy ran to stand beside her.

Chief Talon landed next to Big Ned with a thud. "My friend," he said, reaching out to shake the sheriff's hand. "It is good to see you again."

"Just in time, you old buzzard," Big Ned chuckled.

"Fire away, braves!" Chief Talon screeched.

Artrows flew faster than lightning, twanging as they bombarded the golden statue.

"Great idea," Rumpus exulted, as the enormous golden badger began to soften and sag under the assault.

"Doesn't this remind you of a painting we've seen?" Phlox teased Phil.

The giant golden mayor, melted by artrows into huge blobs of molten gold, slid down, down, faster and faster, and dripped, with huge plops, directly onto the head of the real Mayor Pleasant, matting his fur and holding him in place as it rapidly cooled. The badger was literally trapped in his own greed.

"No, no!" he cried as he struggled in the mess. "Buck! Spratt! You . . . other brother! Help me! No . . . catch them!"

Spratt unleashed his sharp-toothed piranha pistol and Mongo lifted his buzzing battlebee cannon. Both aimed at Big Ned and Chief Talon.

But Bright Eyes took to the air. And as fast as Spratt shot his pistol, the owl, with her blazing-quick hunting skill, plucked each piranha in its flight and hurled it back at Spratt, catching him in the arms and back. He howled, spinning in pain.

Meanwhile, Neddy gently pushed down the nose of the cannon until it faced the ground. Mongo fired, blasting a swarm of angry battlebees at his own feet. He stared at his weapon in utter confusion, as the battlebees buzzed to attack him with their furious stingers. Spratt and Mongo yelped and ran in circles.

"Great work, Bright Eyes!" shouted Big Ned.

"Way to go, Neddy!" shouted Chief Talon.

Phlox, Phil, and Tai smiled in delight at their friends' clever exploits.

But Rumpus had his eye on the last Wildhare who was sneaking away.

"Buck!" Mayor Pleasant appealed, encased in the cooled and hardened gold. "Get me out of this!"

"Every man for himself!" the hare called over his shoulder, as he headed for the west side of town.

Toward the train.

"He's trying to get away!" Rumpus yelled, running. His friends joined him in a mad dash for the station.

"Not if we can stop him!" Phil said, sprinting faster.

Buck loped and hopped at top speed toward the train station, his snake whip trailing behind him. Still, Rumpus, Tai, Phil, and Phlox were gaining on him. They thought he was going to hop the fence to the tracks, but instead, he stopped short right next to the station and dove into a hole in the ground.

"Well that wasn't . . . very smart," said Rumpus, breathing hard. "He has to come out sometime."

The four friends carefully approached the hole. Phil crept to the edge and peeked in.

"Careful of the snake whip," Phlox warned.

"Uh-oh," said Phil, "not good." He looked wildly about.

"What? What is it?" said Tai.

"It's not a hole," Phil said. "It's a tunnel!"

A few seconds later Buck's ears poked out of the ground right next to the end of the train. The rest of his body soon followed as he shot out of the ground. Buck jumped onto the caboose just as the train started to pull away from the station. He spotted the four friends and his moustache curled up wickedly and he let out a satisfied cackle.

"That sneak!" cried Phlox irritably. "That rotten sneak!"

"Here we go again," said Rumpus. He jumped the fence and charged after the train, his three friends right behind. Rumpus threw open the door of one of the boxcars and clambered inside. Phil and Phlox jumped in after him, but Tai kept running.

"Tai, what are you doing?" shouted Rumpus. "Climb in!"

"I have an idea!" Tai answered.

Rumpus, Phil, and Phlox watched as the tiger

picked up speed and swiftly reached the front of the train. With his claws, he latched onto the cab of the locomotive, startling the conductor.

"Sorry!" Tai yelled. "Didn't . . . mean . . . to scare . . . you!" he said between breaths. "But can you . . . please . . . stop . . . the train?!"

In a few moments, the screech of the brakes echoed down the tracks and the train ground to a stop. Tai jogged back to his three friends.

"I did not know you could run like that," panted Rumpus.

"Yeah, you've been holding out on us!" huffed Phil.

"You should join track team if we ever get back to school," wheezed Phlox.

They reached the caboose. Rumpus slowly slid the door open. "I believe this is your stop," he called inside.

Hissss! SNAP! SNAP! Buck's snake whip flew in the air. "Get back you meddlesome kids! You scribbling scoundrels!"

"Scribbling scoundrels . . ." mused Phil. "Hey, I like that!"

"We're not going anywhere," said Tai. "You don't boss anyone in this town anymore."

Even the snake whip seemed to realize Buck's day was over. It slithered from his grip and into the desert.

Back in the town square, Phlox, Phil, Rumpus, and Tai sat the subdued Buck Wildhare down between Mongo and Spratt, who glared at their traitorous brother.

"You did it!" Neddy cheered, trying to wrap all of his friends in a hug with his little arms.

It was only then that Tai saw, peering over Neddy's head, how different the square looked from just that morning. His mouth fell open. There were bright splatters, spots, stripes, and other colorful designs across every wall. Tables and booths had been set up, and the paintings, sculptures, pottery, embroidery, woodwork, and other art the townspeople had smuggled to Pleasant Day were arranged and hung in beautiful displays. War hawks were busy mingling with townspeople and admiring their art.

Rumpus noticed, too. "Wow," he said. "You guys made the mural come to life already!"

Bright Eyes nodded. "Isn't it wonderful? This is just like the old days."

"But that painting . . ." Phil scratched his head. "The one on the cave wall, with the tribe and the town facing off against each other. . . . Does that mean the prophecy is changed? Everyone seems friendly now."

"Remember what Grandmother Buffalo told us?" said Phlox. "Not everything is what it appears. Maybe in that picture they are coming together in determination to defeat a common enemy, not each other."

"Excellent interpretation, Phlox," Bright Eyes agreed.

With Balthazar Pleasant and the Wildhare brothers safe in jail, the townspeople broke out brushes, rollers, and paint and continued to reclaim their town. Blank white walls became canvases. Buildings on every street went from identical to unique—colorful, creative, fantastically varied storefronts expressing their very different individual owners.

"Hey, remember that chameleon with the general store?" said Tai. "He really helped us out when we were on the run. Let's go thank him."

They entered the store and stopped in surprise: The formerly dull interior was a rainbow of hues. And sitting happily behind the counter was the most colorful reptile they had ever seen—the chameleon, blending in perfectly!

When the sun went down in the west that day, the city of Junction was no longer "pleasant," but it was friendly and free. The townspeople celebrated their war hawk allies and the four strangers who had brought the color back into their lives. A potluck feast was laid out for all to share: cream pies, fried pickles, toasted

nuts, even cheese curds—Neddy's favorite.

But Neddy was busy with Bright Eyes. The two friends were designing a fountain together using the owl girl's vases, Neddy's gold pans, and melted gold from the mayor's giant statue. All cheered when it was placed on the pedestal where the statue had stood. "Our first collaboration in a long time," Neddy said happily.

"The first of many," Bright Eyes promised.

Meanwhile, the art festival was in full swing. Bright Eyes surprised Phlox with a beautiful beaded necklace she'd made. Tears filled Phlox's eyes, and she promised her friend she'd write the story of the Claw Foot Tribe in her honor.

Neddy showed Tai how to spin a gold pan. After a few tries, Tai got the hang of it—it was simple angles and geometry, after all. And he only spilt the whole thing twice, which made Neddy burst out laughing.

Rumpus walked around the festival with Big Ned, listening to the little mouse's stories from his time as sheriff: taking down the Wildhare Gang, chasing off cattlefish rustlers, and—Rumpus's favorite—staring down a herd of stampeding hamsters until they stopped in their tracks, just from the look in the sheriff's eye.

Chief Talon and Phil stood on the steps of City Hall, taking it all in. Chief Talon glanced down at the prairie dog. "You scribblers are very brave," he said.

"And you tribespeople are very fierce," Phil replied. "Also, for the record, I dig your whole getup." He gestured to the intimidating, many-feathered, sweeping headdress and war paint. "Very impressive."

Chief Talon preened. "It is rather commanding," he admitted proudly.

Late into the night, exhausted after the eventful day, some townspeople started back to their homes, while others stayed in the town square with their visitors and built a campfire out of old Mayor Pleasant billboards. Chief Talon and Big Ned were in the sheriff's old office hashing out new trade agreements, and Neddy and Bright Eyes sat cozily together by the fire, roasting cubes of cheese.

Phlox and the boys sat around the fire also. What a day! The excitement was wearing off, though. They felt ecstatic about defeating the badger and the Wildhares and reuniting the townsfolk and the tribe, but they couldn't help but feel troubled by one last, very pressing problem: "How do we get home?" Phil asked.

No one had an answer.

Phlox tapped her pencil on her teeth while Tai looked off into the distance, lost in thought.

"We could go back to Grandmother Buffalo at Talking Rock Caves," said Rumpus. "We did promise, after all."

"But what then?" Tai said, his tail waving anxiously.

Phil patted him on the back. "You'll figure it out, Tai. You and Phlox can put the pieces together in the morning, like a mathletics problem."

Phlox squinted as something occurred to her. She got out her notebook and started flipping pages. "Guys!" Phlox held up her notebook. "These are notes I made after Tai and I met the rattle-can snake in the desert. I wanted to capture every detail because it was so mysterious. I wasn't able to make sense of it at the time. After all, we'd just been chased by a pack of your bloodthirsty tumbleweeds . . ." She threw an accusing glare at Rumpus.

"Oh, awesome!" Rumpus looked delighted. "How big were their teeth?"

"Listen," Phlox said, ignoring him, "the snake said something interesting: 'The work isn't finished until it glows. Only then can you see all the pieces. In time help will be given.'"

Tai's eyes sparkled. "'Glow' must refer to the cave paintings. And we helped free the town from the mayor, so our work on the last scene is finished. Do you think that means now we'll be able to see the way home?"

Phlox chewed on her lip. "I don't know . . . the snake was awfully mysterious, wasn't it?"

Phil nodded eagerly. "It's worth a shot. Way to take notes, Phlox."

Phlox grinned and tucked the pencil behind her ear. "My assignment is to get the whole story!"

"Looks like we have our next step," Rumpus declared. "We'll go to the caves and visit Grandmother Buffalo in the morning. From there, we'll figure out what we need to do."

The friends awoke to the cheery bustle of the freshly revived town. Neddy was already busy with his duties in his brand new role as deputy sheriff under his dad, Big Ned, but was still able to supply his friends with hamsters for their journey back across the desert. Bright Eyes, too, had a new responsibility. Chief Talon and Big Ned had agreed that with her wise and peaceable nature she would make an excellent ambassador between the town and the tribe.

Phlox was thrilled for her friends and their exciting new roles, but she wished she and her friends could get back to their lives, too. She decided to rally the boys. It was time to get to the caves and find answers.

In the great chamber of Talking Rock Caves, the mural glowed and shimmered. The adventures of the day before were taking their final form and color. The four friends cracked up when they saw the painting of the mayor covered in his own gold. Rumpus pounded Tai's back in congratulations as they watched the painting of Tai's heroic sprint to the train engine come to life.

"The prophecy is almost complete," said Grandmother Buffalo, beaming at the friends. "You four have done beautifully."

"We still have a problem, though, Grandmother Buffalo," said Phlox. "We don't know how to get home."

"Yes," said Grandmother Buffalo. "That is a bit of a mystery."

"Is there something we're not seeing in the paintings?" asked Tai.

"Keep looking," she answered. "There appears to be one more piece that could use a little color." With that last clue, Grandmother Buffalo turned and left.

"Well, that was worth our coming all this way," said Phil sarcastically.

"I hate to say it," said Tai, "but Phil's right. Grandmother Buffalo wasn't much help. I can't believe she left without helping us."

"Both Grandmother Buffalo and the rattle-can snake seem to be telling us the same thing," said Phlox. "There's something we haven't finished."

Tai ran his fingers over the stampeding cattlefish Rumpus had drawn, the fierce war hawks Phil had imagined, his own golden landscapes. "Everything we three painted in the mural is here," he reflected for a moment. "But what about what Phlox painted?"

"You painted, too, Phlox?" asked Phil.

"Well, I filled in a cactus here and there . . ." she answered thoughtfully. "Oh, and a little sign in the corner."

"A sign?" prompted Rumpus.

Phlox laughed. "Well, it was kind of a joke. It said 'Kansas City, five miles' with an arrow pointing east."

"Everything else we painted is in this world," said Rumpus. "Your sign must be here, too."

The four swept their eyes over the mural, concentrating on the last panel—the painting of the town.

"There!" said Tai suddenly, pointing to the eastern edge of town. "There it is!"

A sign suddenly lit up and the words KANSAS CITY, 5 MILES shone clear as day.

"All right, guys," said Phlox. "Let's go find my sign!"

On the eastern edge of Junction, tucked among a tangle of pigweed, stood Phlox's sign, letters worn by the wind. The four gazed in amazement.

"How could Kansas City be only five miles from here?" asked Rumpus.

"Only way to find out is to follow the arrow," said Phil.

"This could be our last time in Junction," said Tai, looking around at the now-familiar town. "What an adventure!"

"I'm going to miss this place," said Phlox. "Especially our friends."

"Let's make sure we can actually get home before

you get too sad," said Phil. "We might be stuck here forever after all."

"I think we may need guides this one last time," said Tai. He looked at Phlox. "Go find Bright Eyes. I'll ask Neddy."

Neddy and Bright Eyes were more than happy to go along. The six friends had been through a lot together, and it was only right that if this was the way back home, Bright Eyes and Neddy should see them off.

"Good news, Rumpus," said Tai. "This might be our last hamster ride."

"Let's hope so," the rhino muttered. He bounced on his hamster unhappily.

"You all don't have hamsters in Kansas City?" said Neddy in wonderment.

"We do have hamsters," said Phil. "But they fit in the palm of your hand."

"Tiny hamsters . . ." murmured Neddy thoughtfully.

They rode under a brilliant blue sky. Occasion-ally they heard the cry of a war hawk in the distance or passed a herd of grazing cattlefish. The boys admired their handiwork, knowing it could be the last time to see it in person.

Bright Eyes perched on Phlox's hamster and they talked quietly about Phlox's plan to write their adventure and the history of the tribe into a book. "Of course your story will be illustrated, too?" Bright Eyes asked. "After all, you have three artists at your command who saw it all, too."

Meanwhile, Neddy tried to warn the boys, so they wouldn't be too disappointed. "I don't know what we'll find way out here. As far as I've ever heard, it's empty all the way to the big river. Nothing but an old gold panning shop that's been closed a long time."

About five miles past Junction, the small shop appeared.

"Looks like it's back in business!" observed Tai, excited. "And the door is open."

Inside, the shop was full of gold-panning equipment: pans, sieves, and sluice boxes.

"Welcome, folks!" said a large armadillo, smiling broadly. "Come on in to Pat's Gold Pan! I'm Pat."

Neddy let out a long whistle. "You've got some fine tools," he said, picking up a shiny new pan. "I didn't know your shop was in business."

"The badger ran me out when he came to town," said Pat. "But with him in jail, I'm up and running again."

The friends were pleased to hear they had helped this jovial armadillo.

"Plus I get to show my mural again," Pat continued.

"Your mural?" asked Tai.

"Outside, on the wall," the armadillo said. "The mayor made me hide it. Actually, he ordered me to whitewash over it, but I didn't have the heart to do it. Since nobody hardly ever comes over on this side of town, I just covered it." He smiled at his own cleverness. "As soon as I heard the mayor was knocked off his pedestal, so to speak, I took the sheet down."

"Can we see it?" asked Phlox eagerly.

"Of course! I'm mighty proud of it," said Pat. "Although I can't take any credit. It was there when I got here, and nobody knows who painted it or how long ago."

The armadillo led them around the corner of the building (engraved ESTABLISHED 1854) to the large, vibrant, colorful painting on the side wall. The friends caught their breath.

The four friends gazed in awe at the Kansas City they knew so well, with its familiar landmarks and landscape. They'd seen that skyline a million times. It was home.

"Beautiful, isn't it?" asked Pat. "But so mysterious. I mean, obviously, buildings can't be that tall for real."

The soaring skyscrapers of modern Kansas City did look impossible in the flat, empty plains of the Weird Wild West.

"It does seem mysterious," said Phil, "but it's really real. That's where we're from." He touched the wall. Solid. He pushed. Nothing. He banged his fists. "Let us in!" he shouted. "We wanna go home!"

"Easy, Phil," said Rumpus.

"Is that little guy OK?" asked Pat, looking at Phil uncertainly.

"He's just homesick, that's all," answered Rumpus. "We all are."

"Sure." Pat sounded unpersuaded. He headed inside while the friends continued to gaze.

"Boy," said Neddy, "that's quite a town."

"It's no Junction," said Tai, "but it's home."

"And no Talking Rock Caves," said Phlox, "but we have great art of our own."

"I miss our town," Phil moaned. "I miss our buildings, I miss our parents, I even miss our school!"

"This can't be coincidence," said Phlox to Neddy and Bright Eyes. "Our home painted on the side of this building, just like we painted your home on the side of Rumpus's grandpa's building."

"This must be another portal," Bright Eyes agreed. "You just need to find a way through it."

"When we went through the mural last time, the paint was still wet," remembered Tai.

"So all we need is some paint," said Rumpus. "Magic paint . . ."

A spray paint can rattled. Then another.

"Phil, I don't think regular spray paint is going to do it," said Rumpus.

"I'm not touching a thing!" protested Phil, holding up empty hands. The friends turned to see three rattle-can snakes slithering toward them, tails rattling.

"Thissss work issssss unfinished," said one of the snakes. "Issssss it not?"

"Unfinished?" said Tai.

"Yesss," the snake said. "Or elsssse the painting would be glowing."

Now that he mentioned it, the mural did look not quite done. The buildings were plain, there were few details, and corners and backgrounds were empty.

"We'd finish it," said Rumpus. "But we don't have the right kind of paint."

"Sssso you sssssay," the snake said. It slithered to the mural and opened its jaws. With a *psssht*, out sprayed spurts of yellow-gold that shimmered and glowed.

"You're artists, too!" Phil said in awe.

"Of coursse," it said. "We are the original sssscribbler ssssnakes. The painterssssss of Talking Rock Cavesss."

"Now it all makes sense!" said Phlox. Her mind was working quickly, putting together the pieces of the puzzle. "Those squiggly lines all over the cavern paintings—are those your signatures? You snakes painted those murals. You foretold the prophecies."

"And you fulfilled the propheciessss," said the snake. "You ssset thingsss right. Now it issssssss time."

"For what?" asked Tai.

"For help," it said. "In time help will be given, remember? We are the paint. That isssss the help."

The friends got to work, adding detail and color to every inch. With every stroke and spray, it looked more and more like their beloved hometown, while to Bright Eyes and Neddy, the already mysterious mural became even more wonderful.

"Amazing!" said Bright Eyes. "I can't believe what you're painting—those tall, fancy buildings and big bridges and paved roads stretching here and there!"

"We think it's amazing, too," said Phil, "because it's our home."

"I'm going to miss you so much," said Phlox, embracing Bright Eyes and Neddy. "Both of you." She pulled out her camera. "OK, everyone in front!"

This time the boys lined up happily alongside their friends and Phlox snapped away.

Then it was time for the final bit of artwork: Rumpus, Phil, and Tai painted a small building just on the edge of downtown. As soon as Phlox finished the lettering on the sign—DUNCAN'S PLUMBING SUPPLY & SERVICES—the entire mural lit up, glowing and shimmering. And just as suddenly as they had arrived, the three rattle-can snakes slithered away.

"'The work isn't finished until it glows,'" Phlox quoted, watching them disappear into the desert.

"Well, I guess this is good-bye," said Tai to Bright Eyes and Neddy. He placed his paw to the wet mural, making it ripple and shimmer. "It's been a wonderful adventure. Thank you for sharing it with us."

"Quick, before the paint dries!" Phil shouted.

The four friends held hands and jumped.

And just like that, there they were, standing beside Duncan's Plumbing Supply store in the middle of modern-day Kansas City, not a gold-panning supply store in the Weird Wild West.

"Whoo-hoo! Can you believe it?" Phil cried, jumping and spinning in circles and falling to the ground and rolling wildly. "We're back! I thought we'd never make it back!"

Rumpus grinned, happily taking in the skyscrapers in the distance and the music blaring from a passing car.

"Wow." Phlox twirled her pencil. "I'd say I've got quite a job ahead of me — writing the story of a lifetime. And this is no school newspaper story. This is a book!"

Tai breathed a deep sigh of relief. "I'm not saying I didn't have a blast in the Wild West we invented," he said, "but it was really, really weird. And it is very nice to be back."

"That's not all that's nice!" Phil jumped up, remembering. "Wait till you see this!"

His friends raised their eyebrows. "What now, Phil?"

"We're rich!"

Very dramatically, Phil reached into his pocket and pulled out a hand: "Ta-da!"

Silence.

After a moment, Phlox burst into laughter. Rumpus and Tai snorted as Phil stared in horror: Gold paint coated his fingers and dripped down his palm.

"But . . . but . . ." Phil stammered in shock. "These were solid gold nuggets! Big ones!"

"And where did you get those nuggets, Phil?" Phlox said between giggles.

"I found them!" he argued. "They were mine, fair and square! What happened to my gold?!"

Tai tried to take his friend's consternation seriously, but he couldn't help but laugh. "Consider this theory: That world was made of paint. So it stands to reason that things from that world—like nuggets of gold—would return to their original state when we crossed back into this world."

"Oh, now you tell me." Phil looked down at his dripping hands, scowling. "Think how much gold that was going to be! Thousands of dollars worth!"

"Didn't we just learn the evil of greed?" Phlox teased.

"You're supposed to be painting the mural," a familiar voice chuckled, "not yourselves."

"Grandpa!" Rumpus rushed to the old rhino, giving him a huge hug. "Finally!"

"Finally?" Grandpa Horn gave a puzzled smile. "You've only been out here a couple of hours. I thought I'd see if you wanted some lemonade—it can get pretty hot out here."

"You have no idea!" Phil muttered as he remem-bered riding their hamsters through the dry desert heat.

But Grandpa Horn was admiring their mural. "Looks good, you kids," he said. "I really like how you brought everything together."

Phlox and the boys turned to the mural . . . and stared in amazement.

It was totally changed. The three artists' very different sections were now merged into one, creating a busy, thrilling scene that meshed seamlessly together, yet still showcased the particular talents of each individual artist. Rumpus's cattlefish roamed across Tai's beautiful plains. They were chased by Phil's cowboys on free-range hamsters, Big Ned and Neddy leading the way. Chief Talon, Bright Eyes, and the war hawks soared above them. Phlox's Kansas City sign was now planted front and center and a lovely beaded necklace—an exact replica of the one Bright Eyes had given her—hung from a corner.

"I was hoping for a lot from you kids, but this is even more impressive than I expected," Grandpa Horn said. "I wouldn't be surprised if you get calls from other business owners wanting their own murals after they see this fine piece." He watched them out of the corner of his eye, and it seemed like he was holding back a sly smile. "I have plenty of that paint. You're welcome to use it if you get any future commissions." Chuckling, Grandpa Horn went back inside.

Tai, Rumpus, Phlox, and Phil grinned at each other.

"We need a name for ourselves," Phlox said. "If we're going to be doing more murals together, we better be called something. I'll put it in my story, to get us known, you know?"

Tai paused. He thought of Neddy, and what he'd called them after they finished their work on the mural on the side of City Hall that night before the festival, and what the mysterious spray-can snakes had called themselves. "What about . . . the Scribblers?"

"What about the Scribble Squad?" Phlox suggested. "Because we do art and we do it together."

"I like it!" Phil said. "Makes us sound like an adventure team."

"Like a cross between an art club and a band of superheroes," Rumpus agreed.

"Scribble Squad it is!" Phlox wrote it in block letters on the cover of her notebook.

Rumpus signed the mural with their new name:

"Now . . ." Phil sighed, looking at his messy hands and the gold he'd had—literally—right at his fingertips. "I could really use some lemonade."

"Hear, hear!" Tai seconded.

Rumpus slung his backpack over his shoulder. Phil and Tai picked up Grandpa Duncan's special paint cans and headed into the plumbing store. Phlox followed, but stopped as she noticed the date engraved on the worn old cornerstone: ESTABLISHED 1854.

Phlox whistled. "Well, I'll be. I wonder . . ." She took out her notebook, writing faster and faster as she walked around the corner.

WHERE & WHEN WAS THE WILD WEST?

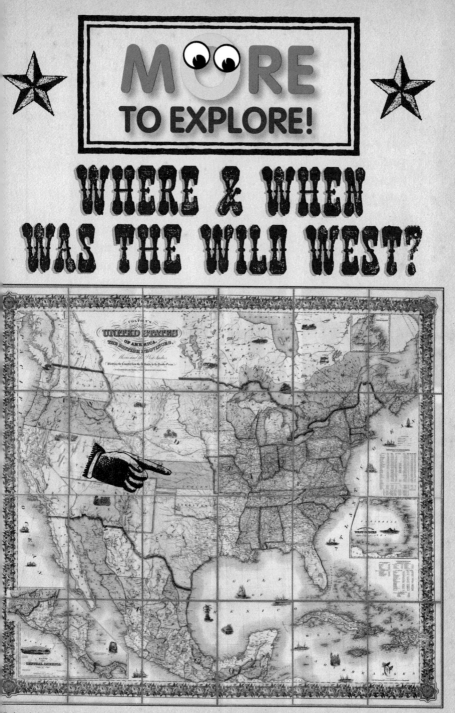

Colton's Map of the United States of America, The British Provinces, Mexico and The West Indies Showing the Countries from the Atlantic to the Pacific Ocean . . . . 1854 (Note the date: 1854. Sound familiar?)

WHERE

Many of the most famous events of the "Wild West" took place in what we now call the *Midwest*—in states like Oklahoma, Nebraska, Kansas, and Missouri. Carved out of the vast territory bought from France by President Thomas Jefferson in the Louisiana Purchase, these states were wild compared to the older, settled areas east of the Mississippi River.

WHEN

Many historians date the start of the Wild West to the rise of Jesse James in the late 1860s, just after the Civil War. It ended in the 1890s, with the takedown of the Dalton Gang in 1892 and the Wild Bunch by 1898. But thanks to the popularity of Western novels and movies, the Wild West lives on.

LAWMEN

The Wild West was known for lawlessness. With a lot of territory and few lawmen, outlaws could get away with a lot. Keeping criminals in line was a dangerous job, as Big Ned would tell you.

Wyatt Earp

Famous for: the gunfight at the O.K. Corral, one of the best-known shootouts in the history of the Wild West—though it only lasted about 30 seconds.

Wild Bill Hickok

Famous for: the duel against Davis Tutt in the streets of Springfield, Missouri. It was the first recorded "quick draw" duel, with two gunmen facing each other and drawing their pistols as fast as they could.

Bill Tilghman

Famous for: capturing renowned outlaw Bill Doolin in Arkansas without firing a single shot.

OUTLAWS

While many people considered outlaws to be villains, others saw them as celebrities. Small, cheap books called "dime novels" (because they were sold for a dime) were full of colorful adventures and very popular, with stories about outlaws some of the most popular of all.

Billy the Kid

Infamous for: the Battle of Lincoln, a gunfight that lasted over four days. He wasn't really a "kid"—he was nineteen years old—but he wasn't a full-grown man either, and people described him as looking like a young schoolboy.

Belle Starr

Infamous for: being the "Queen of the Oklahoma Outlaws." She was known for her crack-shot aim with a

pistol and cattle-rustling schemes, which landed her in a Michigan prison for nine months.

Jesse James

Infamous for: his success as a bank, train, and stagecoach robber with his brother, Frank James. The Jesse James Gang originated in the Kansas City area (hometown of the Scribble Squad!) and robbed banks, stagecoaches, and other businesses in Kansas City and nearby towns. In their first train robbery in 1873, the Gang stole $3,000—about $60,000 today.

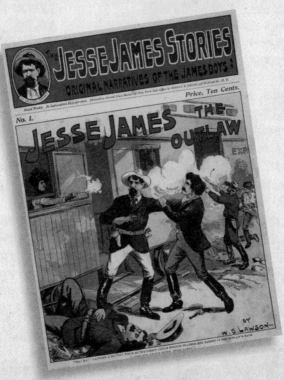

LANDSCAPE OF THE WEST

Newspaper Rock is one of the largest collections of petroglyphs, or picture-symbols, in the United States. The first marks were carved around 2,000 years ago and include images of pronghorn antelope and riders on horseback, as well as depictions of past events, just like a newspaper! The Navajo name for the rock is Tse' Hane, which means "rock that tells a story." If they were around, Bright Eyes and Phlox could help decipher some of these stories.

Antelope Canyon is a deep, narrow canyon created from years of running water and erosion. It is famous for its dramatic spiral arches, flowing walls, and twisting curves— can you imagine the epic war hawk chases through canyons like these?

Sometimes called "chicken hawks," **Cooper's hawks** are swift birds of prey. The females are actually larger than the males. Their red-orange eyes are particularly sharp, and like other hawks, they can spot and catch their prey while flying at top speeds. Nowadays, you might even see them in cities, hunting for pigeons, but these hunters are right at home in our story as fierce war hawks.

It might seem tricky to tell the difference between **hares** and rabbits, but a few things that set them apart. While rabbits live underground, hares make their homes in flattened nests aboveground. And hares are larger than rabbits, with longer hind legs that help them run at 40 miles per hour—no wonder the Wild-hare Gang was so difficult to catch.

Prairie dogs are herbivores, meaning that they eat plants: lots of grasses, flowering plants, roots, and seeds. These rodents have short tails and make a gruff sound when danger is nearby. They are native to the plains region, so Phil and Phlox are right at home in Kansas City. The Lewis and Clark Expedition, which first mapped the newly purchased Louisiana Territory in the early 1800s, encountered prairie dogs and wrote about them in their journals. Meriwether Lewis called them "barking squirrels." What would Phil and Plox have to say about that?

True to its name, the **desert pocket mouse** is no more than seven inches long when full-grown. These rodents head underground to make their homes, preferring the soft soil along stream bottoms. They're excellent diggers, which might be why Neddy has such a knack for finding gold.

Burrowing owls are known for their bright, gleaming eyes, long legs, and the unusual location of their nests—underground! They make their homes in holes that have already been made by other desert critters (like prairie dogs). These small owls mostly hunt rodents at night, meaning Bright Eyes and Neddy certainly make an odd couple.

Andrews McMeel Publishing
a division of Andrews McMeel Universal
1130 Walnut Street, Kansas City, Missouri 64106

www.andrewsmcmeel.com

16 17 18 19 20 SDB 10 9 8 7 6 5 4 3 2 1

ISBN: 978-1-4494-6921-4

Library of Congress Control Number: 2016935675

Editor: Grace Suh
Creative Director: Tim Lynch
Production Editor: Erika Kuster
Production Manager: Chuck Harper
Written by: Mariah Marsden and Brandi Handley
With contribution by: Josh Elder

Made by:
Shenzhen Donnelley Printing Company Ltd.
Address and location of manufacturer:
No. 47, Wuhe Nan Road, Bantian Ind. Zone,
Shenzhen China, 518129
1st Printing—6/13/16

Colton's Map of the United States of America, The British Provinces,
Mexico and The West Indies on page 245 provided by
www.RareMaps.com—Barry Lawrence Ruderman Antique Maps Inc.

Pocket mouse image on page 255 provided by Bob Beatson

ATTENTION: SCHOOLS AND BUSINESSES
Andrews McMeel books are available at quantity discounts with bulk purchase for
educational, business, or sales promotional use. For information, please e-mail the
Andrews McMeel Publishing Special Sales Department: specialsales@amuniversal.com.